ALL the THINGS WE DO in the DARK

SAUNDRA MITCHELL

HarperTeen is an imprint of HarperCollins Publishers.

All the Things We Do in the Dark

www.epicreads.com

Library of Congress Control Number: 2019937377
ISBN 978-0-06-285260-1

Typography by Torborg Davern
21 22 23 24 25 PC/LSCH 10 9 8 7 6 5 4 3 2 1

First paperback edition, 2021

FOR PHIL:

MY BIGGEST, MOST UNEXPECTED, PROUDEST FAN.

THIS ONE IS FOR YOU, DAD.

This novel discusses sexual assault and sexual violence, and contains depictions of non-sexual violence and PTSD that may be triggering to survivors. Please see page 296 for help and resources for sexual-abuse and assault survivors.

last, there is nothing: the nothing between sleeping and waking, the not-being, not-feeling, not-knowing of anesthesia with no count-backwards-from-ten-nine-eight—

leftover, a heat too small to warm the sky; instead the sky drinks heat until muscles tighten, fingers stiffen, blood settles. the earth drinks, the river sighs, the trees watch—

one in particular, the half-oak: it closes like the lid of a music box. it folds the girl beneath its shelter; it protects the strange jewel inside from all predators but one—

her eyes are open
she does not sleep

HOW DO I TELL YOU ABOUT THE BODY?

I'm gonna start with the worst thing that ever happened to me.

In summer; I was nine. Flip-flops, jorts, and my favorite green Minecraft T-shirt. I rode my red-white-and-blue bike around and around our apartment complex until I was primed with dirt and sweat—

For the record, I'm going back so far, from then to now, because it's not a straight line. Life never is; at least, it hasn't been so far.

So okay. I'd dropped my bike in the grass and sprawled out next to it. Dying in the sun, you know, basically hot-dirty-sweaty, played-out. The grass was cool and sweet and a little bit prickly.

He—tall, like my dad, curly hair like my dad—cast a shadow on me.

"Hey," he said, "I have something that'll keep you cool in the summer."

I negotiated. (Because he was a stranger and *Stranger! Danger!* But also I'm not supposed to be rude to my elders. So which one is he? A stranger? An elder? Neither? Both?) I said, "I only want to look at it."

He told me *it* was down a narrow lane running between the apartments and a strip of trees. It was always cool down there, always a little dark.

After, blood streaked down my cheek. Sweat too, smeared with dirt, sticky with snot. Something else was wet, somewhere else I didn't want to say. *Stranger Danger* said *this was all my fault*, so I slunk home. I had to clean up. I had to hide the cut on my face. I had to peel off my skin and hide so nobody would ever find me again.

Another man followed me home. (*Danger! Danger! Danger!*) From his upstairs window, he'd seen *something*. Enough that he managed to get outside in time to trail me to my back door. I tried to make him go away. I tried, I *tried*, but he wouldn't leave until I got my mom.

I gave up. I was tired.

He talked to my mom, who talked to the police, who talked to me at the hospital after the doctors talked around me and behind me and over me. The same doctors glued the cut on my face closed, like I was a teacup with a new handle, like I was a glitter project.

The gash streaked through my eyebrow, down my cheek, almost to the corner of my mouth. The doctors worried about it getting infected. (They don't understand how it happened. It doesn't make sense the way I explained it. *He had a razor blade finger. He just traced it down my cheek and told me to go home.*)

After that, I wore pants and extra underpants; I wore a hoodie over my T-shirt even when the thermometer topped ninety degrees. I grew my hair long, and I learned to love the inside.

Trees near buildings became bad places, full of poisonous magic.

I love corners; when you sit in one, there's no one behind you.

I love walls that stretch to ceilings; not a seam or crack to be seen.

I love windows; they're where the light comes in.

Only the light.

NORMAL PEOPLE DON'T INTRODUCE THEMSELVES like this, I know. But the scar's right there. It's the signpost that whispers with scandal. It says, *Guess what happened to* ***her***.

These days, I wear one pair of underwear and whatever I feel like over them. I dye my hair into rainbows and cut it into sharp, short angles; the bob edge traces my cheek, the color glimmers. It makes people look away, at least at first, from the scar. But I'm telling *you* so you don't have to guess.

What happened was bad enough; the guessers like to embroider. Sickos, seriously.

Also, I'm saying it because I think I have a responsibility: I had a "good" rape. The kind where I was young enough that it was definitely not my fault. I was not sexy enough for people to think I might have secretly wanted it. My rape was committed by a psycho-stranger-bad-man-not-anybody-nice-we-know.

Extremely not my fault.

Of course, it is *never* anyone's fault.

I just have a story that liars and cheats and skeptics and haters of girls can't argue with. There's no world, no planet, on which a nine-year-old should learn about sex and syphilis in an emergency room while an intern glues her face back together.

I'm obligated to say it out loud for everyone who can't. For the ones who don't have bulletproof stories even though we're all equal: something evil happened, and it happened *to* us. We didn't make the evil happen.

Without the scar, maybe I wouldn't tell my story. It's not exactly a choice: the scar says I have to. That's what introduces me. No matter where I go—to school, to camp, no matter how ordinary-average I am or pretend to be—

I'm that *what happened to her?!* girl.

If we ever have a conversation, I usually get to tell them my name is Ava—*after* I explain the scar. After.

SO I'M DONE TALKING ABOUT THAT NOW.

You know what everybody wants to know. The scar won't distract you anymore, so we can move forward.

I'm getting to it. The body. I'm getting there, all right? But first.

When I tell you what happened, sometimes you're going to want to know, *Does she do that because of* that? Is fill-in-the-blank *behavior* directly related to that *day* when she was nine? And the answer is:

YES

and

NO.

Why did *you* pick that shirt instead of another one? Why'd *you* let your friend be a douche-wagger just a little bit longer than you should have?

I have damage, you have damage. Nobody knows what they're doing while they're doing it.

Maybe yoga masters do. Or Buddhist monks.

Or maybe they forget too. Maybe they just have the veggie dog with relish even though they hate relish because the vendor seemed really nice and invested in sweet, pickled greenness.

It just *is*. I just *am*; you are too. So all of this defensive posturing is basically a way of saying:

What happens later, with the body, is not *because*.

Maybe it's *in spite of.*

And yeah, I'm damaged. Who isn't broken and bleeding right now, really? We all sing along to the strung-out and screwed-up *who-loves-you-because-nobody-loves-me* songs on the radio. And I know in those moments that I'm ugly, I'm worthless, nobody's ever going to look at this and go, *Ohhhh yeah, baby, get into my life.*

And other times . . . other times I am the world. I am the universe and who *wouldn't* want all this? Who's even good enough for it? Not you and not you and not him and not her. I'm flavor walking; I'm the queen, I'm the stars and the sun, and I can fly.

(Sometimes on the same day.)

(Sometimes in the same hour.)

I used to spend a lot of time twisting things up and down and backward, trying to break logic. Or make logic of myself.

Like, here's a question: Am I a virgin?

Don't get squirrelly. You don't have to answer.

My friend Syd, short for Sydney, thinks virginity is stages: mouth virginity, hand virginity—even boyginity and girlginity, with all the subcategories that go with. She *says* she's only being linguistically precise. But her eyebrows have *connotations.*

This is all bull, they say, *so let's take this flawed logic to its most absurd conclusion.*

I don't speak in eyebrows. What I know is that, according to nine-tenths of the population, I'm either chewed bubble gum or absolutely pristine. It depends on the person talking. On the day. The hour. The minute. Who knows for certain?

No one.

I'm Schrödinger's hymen.

ALL THIS TO SAY, I'M NOT AFRAID OF PEOPLE. I JUST don't like them.

I mean, they're fine individually, but I don't like to be marooned in the middle of an ocean full of them. Too many voices, smells, touches—

So I bet you can guess how much I like school-the-place.

I stay on the edges when I'm there so I can meet *my* people, one at a time. That way, everything falls into a pattern and it's just regular. In this class, I talk to *her*; in that class, to *him*—their faces fill out fixed places in my universe.

And that lets me notice new things instantly, like the weekend Syd switched her gold cheek stud for silver, or today, when she's suddenly carrying her bag on her left arm instead of her right.

Her hair won't be tamed, and the ringlets that used to be blond are a silvery blue. The color makes her blue eyes leap out, like she's made from lapis and sapphires and wishes. There, on her wrist, she has new ink.

Possessive, I catch her hand so I can examine her skin. She

went without me. She picked a design *without me.* It feels like a barb, but I try to be happy for her, and it comes out sideways. "You didn't say!"

She shrugs. "It's better in person."

I trace my gaze over the permanent lines still tender and scabbed from their application. Three beehives sit on a bench, perfect golden domes. A haze of bees circles them; they swirl, they dip. Everything is touched with color, shades of tea and tan and honey.

Like the rest of Syd's tattoos, it's medieval. As in, *actually* medieval. Images from rare manuscripts illuminate her shoulders and her wrists, her ankles and her hips.

We've bonded over many things, and the distant past is one of them. (I like school-the-learning just fine; Syd and I own the history department.)

"Tacuinum," she says cryptically but not. That's the name of the manuscript where she found her bees. Every time she gets new ink, she catalogs it for me. *Luttrell*, *Tacuinum*, *Etymologiae.* She wears the history she loves on her skin; I keep mine in my head.

None of my tattoos belong to me; other people wore them first. I have Gaga's Rilke quote on the inside of my arm and Lana del Rey's *paradise* on the side of my foot. Rihanna's stars cascade across my hip; Cara Delevingne's wasp stings my shoulder.

These tattoos belong to people who are free and abundantly themselves. When they walk in, they belong, even though they look like they came from the moon or Mars or the Milky Way.

They don't have scars; they *are* the scar—the line that separates them from the ordinary is their entire existence.

Their tattoos are my icons, little etched Patronus charms that fly across my body. So when I get ink, I get theirs. I reach for what they have; I cling to it in permanent colors.

"This is my favorite," I tell Syd, allowing myself one last brushing touch against her wrist. Do I sound wistful? Resentful? I don't think so; maybe I do. Uncertain, I add, "I like it better than the poppies, even."

Syd smiles and falls into step with me. "Ooh, better than the poppies? Are you sure? Do you feel okay?"

"Shut up." I lean into her. Maybe I had gushed about the poppies more than once, but they're amazing. They grow over the curve of her shoulder and drape along the angle of her collarbone.

They're perfect and she's taunting me. I would elbow her, but we're already pressed together, a needle to thread the crowded school halls.

"I picked it out in June; just now got the money for it."

"Seriously? June? Shut up!"

A decision made when we were a million miles apart; it figures. We used to spend summers together; now we just miss each other for June and July. I go to my dad's. She stays and lives a whole nother life, apparently.

I say, "I was stuck listening to dad jokes, and you were picking out tats. You suck."

"I do," she replies. "That's why all the boys like me."

I snort. The girls like her too . . . as do all the people who are between, or both or neither. Let's simplify: humans with a pulse.

They like Syd, and she likes them back, fearlessly. Maybe I should get one of Syd's tattoos.

"Heart eyes, every direction," I say. "Must be nice."

"People like you," she says. Then she makes a sound—*tch*—and shrugs it off.

It's a conversation we've had a million times; it never goes anywhere. It's contained in a bubble. I like plenty of people—humans with a pulse, actually—as long as they're far away and, in their distance, untouchable. Syd doesn't always have the patience for constructed unrequitedness, so she changes the subject.

"Guess what. Stepdork gave me twenty bucks for no reason."

"You have a job."

"I know, right? But twenty bucks."

"So now you can take Meghan to get fondue."

The fondue is a joke—there's this pit right outside Caribou with nothing but fondue. Like, nobody goes there; I have literally never seen a car there, but the OPEN sign is always on. So we all joke about how it's the most romantic restaurant in Maine.

Syd makes a zero with her hand and holds it up between us. That's her sign that the hooking up with Meghan didn't quite hook—and won't ever again.

"I'm sorry," I say instantly, but I feel off balance and awkward. Syd usually tells me things in the moment; she texts me the second anything good, bad, or indifferent happens.

As her best friend, I'm not supposed to stumble into conversational minefields. I should already know . . . about the ink, about the girl. Even though I feel the heat from her body against mine, she's just out of reach. And why? What did I do? What have I done?

I rack my brain and try to find some offense that would send Syd off into the atmosphere, away from me. But there's nothing. I can't think of anything, not even a text with no punctuation. So I do what I'm supposed to do. I comfort. I sympathize. "That sucks. I know you really liked her."

"Whatever. It's all good."

Syd seems okay—genuinely. (I'm the one who's off.)

(I usually am.)

See, most of the time, Syd's a transient when it comes to romance. She doesn't plan where she's going, and she doesn't stay all that long.

The only serious relationship she's had was with Connor; her boyginity was involved.

The week after, he told her he needed to go out with other people for *reasons*. Not good reasons or specific reasons; just because. He wouldn't even take the blame. It wasn't him, it was her.

And so Syd packed up her heart, learned to hang, and found Amber, who's willing to tattoo us in her warehouse apartment, underage, if we pay in cash.

When we went for our tattooginity, Syd got a pair of blue demon legs with the devil's face for the butt on her arm (*Luttrell*), and I got a swallow etched into my back (Ruby Rose).

Syd always makes herself bigger, scarier, stronger with everything she does. Her hair. Her clothes. Her ink.

People look at me and back away. (The scar.)

The more Syd modifies, the more that's true for her, too.

We share an orbit, spinning and spinning around an unnamed planet—dark side, light side, always in tandem. We fit. We go. We're safe.

Or we used to be.

Now she's hiding things from me.

I'LL BE LATE, **MY MOTHER TEXTS.** USE THE CARD.

My mother is often late. I often use the card to order pizza or Chinese or sandwiches. Emphasis on the order: I'm not supposed to go out without prior authorization.

Actually, that makes it sound like Mom chains me in the house. It's not like that. It's a soft expectation. If she doesn't take me to the place or explicitly give me permission to be in the place, well, I'm not supposed to be at the place.

If I *asked* to stay the night with Syd, no problem, permission granted. If I asked to go anywhere—well, probably, the answer was yes. She'd take me; Mom and I go to the library, we go bowling, we go swimming.

Just never me on my own. It's for the best, though.

A couple of years ago, I tried to go to summer camp. I picked it myself: Camp Sweetwater, near the Hirundo Wildlife Refuge. It was supposed to be three weeks of intensive, hands-on history and archaeology, complete with trenches and test pits. (No real archaeology would have been harmed in the making of this trip.)

I bailed in the first week. It was too much. Too many people asking about the scar or, worse, not asking about it and *staring*. Hands framing mouths don't keep in the whispers; they just make it obvious that people are whispering, about *you*.

The whole place was dangerous to my skin. The open bunks felt like threats; the open showers like invasions. We were supposed to huddle in the morning, trust fall in the afternoon, share tools, touch hands, shoulders to shoulders, strangers, strangers, strangers.

I tried for five days, cried every single one of those days, then came home. As I stepped out of my first shower in almost a week, I heard my mom arguing with my dad on speaker.

"There's no point asking for a refund, Tony. It's right there in all the paperwork: no refunds."

"They can't make an exception?"

"They *won't*."

"It was fifteen hundred bucks," Dad sniped. "You could at least ask."

"You do it. Feel free."

"I think she should go back. She's going to turn into a basket case."

"Tony . . ."

"One of those people who never leave the house."

"Okay, I'm done. She leaves the house. She's fine."

"Yeah, it sounds like it."

I leave the house, I thought. *All the time.* Usually with Mom, yes. Sometimes with Syd, yes. With anyone else? I mean, almost never, but so? I could if I wanted to. And between Mom and Syd, I see all the movies, buy all the books, and get all the tattoos I need.

(And you know what? When I go to Dad's house in the summer, you know what I do? Read books and text Syd and mess around on the internet. Dad and I go out to dinner, and then we go home. Dad isn't big on the library, and I'm not interested in fishing/war movies/physics documentaries/heirloom tomatoes. So there. I mean, seriously, so there, right in his face.)

I use the card; I order pizza. And I'm fine, by myself, in my own house, in my own bed. *Actually* fine, not defensive fine. I don't double-triple-quadruple check to see if anything is locked. Weird noises don't bother me; I've learned the songs of our house. Of our neighborhood. They're not mysteries. Wood thrushes, mockingbirds, foxes, the Nguyens' shed door, the ice maker refilling.

When I'm by myself at home, it's a girl, her laptop, and her own large pepperoni pizza: a love story.

I am not a basket case.

WHAT DOES THIS HAVE TO DO WITH ANYTHING?

Everything.

Some questions have easy answers. Baby math, like two plus two: four. Why did you eat the last ice cream sandwich? Because I wanted it. Don't you want to go to your dad's for the summer? No, not particularly.

You can stripe a life out in primary colors: who's your best friend, where do you go to school, what makes you gag (Syd, Aroostook High North, thinking about stuff touching people's eyes).

But the shades between there, you have to get there to describe them. So if you ask me *why* Syd is my best friend, I have to tell you that our moms were in a baby group together. But I also have to tell you it's Syd punching Becker in kindergarten when he licked my apple slice and made me cry. It's me baking Syd yellow cake–chocolate icing cupcakes for her eighth birthday.

She only ever asked me once if the cut on my face hurt. Everything else she knows—even details I didn't tell my mom—she knows because I volunteered.

So before the body I have to tell you about the fight that isn't a fight.

To tell you *how* it happens, I have to tell you what happened before. This is one of those easy things, and I'm not being smart or trying to avoid the question or anything like that. It's just that the alphabet goes A-B-C, not A-F-Z.

I'm getting there.

SUNDAY NIGHT, IT SNOWS.

It's only October, but it's not a shock or anything. It happens here sometimes.

Syd and I used to go trick-or-treating in the snow when we were kids. My mom piled us into the car and drove us from house to house. She blasted the heater the whole time. We'd toast up, then surge over walks to front doors decorated with pumpkins and icicles, then run back to the heat again to compare candy.

Thinking about it now, it makes me wonder why we even dressed up. I can't remember a Halloween without a coat on, ever. I could have been a princess or a stormtrooper or a princess stormtrooper, for all anybody could see under my layers.

But this morning, the crackle of brand-new snow against gold and scarlet leaves feels like bad luck. Pulling on thicker socks, I stare out my bedroom window. Huge white fluffs drift down, absurdly large, big as birds' eggs, light as feathers.

This isn't the order of things. (It feels the same as finding out about Syd's breakups and tattoos after the fact: everything is the wrong way around. Slightly off.)

I finish dressing for cold. The thermostat at school is on a schedule, and it's still gonna be set for pleasant fall, not sudden winter.

The bus is late. (They haven't changed to the all-weather tires yet, the ones they can chain up if they have to.) The roads are clearish, but people drive like they'd never seen winter before. Skids and stops and horns and slow, slow turns. Every couple of blocks, somebody's off the road in a ditch.

The dark, shadowy side I keep under my skin finds it kinda funny when it's an SUV. Like, they thought they could beat Maine and Mother Nature with four-wheel drive? What are they, new?

Then my stomach clenches when I see a car like my mother's off the road, in the tree line. Long skid marks spirograph through the snow, revealing mud and green grass beneath the swirls. Yellow hazard lights flash, but the inside of the car is dark.

Craning my neck, I watch it disappear behind us. It's the wrong color. I press my blunt nails into my palm and swear to myself. Not her. Not her. Wrong color.

(She texts me from work. It's not her. She's fine.)

AT SCHOOL, THE HALLS ARE TOO CROWDED.

Excited voices compete with slamming lockers, and cold wind blasts down the corridors. It's gonna be one of those days with shoes soaking wet and dark streaks climbing the hems of our jeans. The first bell hasn't even rung, and everything already has a slushy-dirty kind of tinge.

I shoulder between people to get to my locker, and my skin crawls. It prickles and recoils, beneath my coat, beneath my sweater. Everybody's in the way; why can't they get out of the way?

It's just snow. We see it every year! Too much of it every year! Why people have to pack the halls and breathe all the air and fill up all the space because of it, I don't know. Bodies graze behind mine; I clench my teeth.

All these strangers touching me. An electrical tension tightens inside me. I want to hit them all, bash them all out of the way. But I can't; I can't hit people for taking up space, even though I'm reasonably sure I could come up with a reason why I should. Before that thought lingers too long, I realize *I can bail.*

But I don't really know how to do it. I'm a good student—on

track for a couple of scholarships. I mean, I'm not even sure I'm going to ditch on Senior Skip Day, and that's a year away and parent-approved.

It's time for school, so I have to be at school. Those are the rules.

But I have to escape.

I squeeze my eyes closed against threatening tears, and I try not to think about it. About the people near me, invading.

With a slam, I close my locker and make myself small. *Escape, escape.* Arms around me, tight, tight, tight, and head down, shoulders first, I burrow through the crowd to get to the library. Nobody's going there before first period.

Bursting through the media center doors, I breathe, finally. I draw deep: cool air fills me up and inflates me again. I stand there, between the bars of the security scanner that have stopped no one from stealing the good manga from the shelves.

Again, I breathe. Okay. I'm good. I'm fine.

The doors swing open behind me, and I skitter out of the way. When I turn back to look, I see Hailey Kaplan-Cho, wearing a Hufflepuff hat and a smile.

"Ava," Hailey says, a laugh in her voice. "I didn't mean to scare you. I guess you didn't hear me coming."

I hadn't heard her, not even a little. It's embarrassing, my fear of otherwise harmless situations. It's also disappointing. People never notice all that panic in me. From the outside, I look normal.

I drag myself back to okay and manage a smile. "Yeah, sorry; it's crazy out there, right?"

"Completely. They act like they've never seen snow before." Hailey shrugs; she has no idea she read my mind. "Anyway, you dropped this."

In her hand, my glove.

"Thanks," I say as I take it. "I didn't realize. Obviously."

"No problem," she says, and sweeps the hat off her head. Strands of her hair defy gravity, trailing coppery-bronze into the air. She sweeps a self-conscious hand over it. Her hair drifts free again, unconcerned.

She asks, "Did you have a good summer?"

We literally know each other so little that this is a reasonable question to ask in October.

"Had to go stay with my dad," I say. "He lives near Mount Desert."

"That sounds nice."

I would tell her it isn't, but I've learned the hard way that telling the absolute truth ruins a conversation. My bones jolt and tick, warning me not to ruin *this* conversation. *Don't back away; don't be awkward. God, I'm so awkward.* I say, "It was all right. What about you?"

"Pretty good," she says cheerfully. "Got my license, finally!"

"Yay!"

"Right?" Her smile blazes bright, a blush darkening her cheeks. "And Dad finally let me get a job outside of his office. That was kind of amazing."

"Oh yeah? Where at?"

"The library; I'm a page. It's not super exciting or anything. I don't have a desk, but I don't have to listen to the drunk tank the whole time, either."

I forgot that Hailey's dad is a cop. A detective, actually. Somewhere in time, I'd known it, and when she mentions it, the thin glass cracks and memories squeeze through.

My mom closed the door between me and her; she stood on the front porch and talked to Officer Cho. He was the first. Then came the many; how many cops does it take to get to the center of a disaster?

His face doesn't float up from the murk. There were too many uniforms and too many people and just too many everything, to be specific. But he's connected; one stitch in my scar.

I bet Hailey knows all about it. Or maybe not. Or maybe?

I have to cut off the loop in my head, or this is all I'll think about all afternoon. I should deploy another thought. One from the present, one that is pleasant.

I wonder what kind of job Hailey had at the police department. Was it a real job, or was her dad keeping an eye on her? Because he knew what happened to me. Because he saw.

New thought, Ava!

A new job, she's happy, so I celebrate with her. For her, I guess. I hear my lips say something dumb: "Woo hoo, freedom!"

"All the freedom! All for me!" Her laughter is soft and kind of indulgent.

God, she's just being polite. This whole morning has me frazzled and acting like a (basket case) space ranger or something.

I'm not usually like this.

It's just the wrong snow and not my mother's car in a ditch

and all the people in the halls and I'm—off. And she can tell. So I make myself say more words, more stupid words as my mouth goes dry.

"But now we're back in school," I say. "Booooooo."

She laughs again—it sounds realer. "Boo for real. Bring back summer, already."

"The one whole day of it we get a year," I joke.

"Exactly."

When we go quiet, it's not silence. The halls are too loud for that; the clock on the wall ticks off seconds until our first block starts. Another dizzy, awkward wave rolls through me. I don't know what else to say to her. I don't not want to talk to her—but now it feels like I've thought about it too long. It's my turn, and I've got nothing.

I blurt out, "I, sorry, I need to get to my locker before the bell rings."

"Oh," she says. She dims, then she nods. "Me too."

"Thanks again," I tell her, waving my glove in her direction. Manners are automatic.

Hailey pushes the doors open for me. As I pass, she says, "No problem."

Her perfume smells like cedar and citrus.

MR. BURKHART'S CLASS IS A MUSEUM OF MAPS.

They line the walls, some of them hanging, some pinned with thumbtacks. (Clear thumbtacks, so clever. *Where does he find them?* I always wonder.) Mercator Projection, Boggs-Eumorphic, Natural Earth—posters and plastic projections where the mountains rise up to meet your fingers.

But most important, chronological. If you start at the door and walk around the room, you can see the world change in cartography over time. Roman empire, Byzantine empire—above those, dynasties: Xia flows to Shang to Zhou.

It's a flipbook in slow motion, ending in a modern map with unions instead of empires, a separate Serbia from Bosnia, the world now as we know it. Sort of.

The pieces keep shifting across the Atlantic, but the drift is so small and so far from Maine, that things feel permanent to me. Puerto Rico as a state? The glimmer of a dream. Catalan independence? Not if the Spanish can help it. So this map without those seismic shifts, this is my world.

"So let's think about this in perspective," Mr. Burkhart says without preamble. "Richard III's death on Bosworth Field *could* be considered the beginning of the American experiment. Seven years before Columbus sailed the ocean blue, a hundred and twenty-two years before Jamestown, almost three hundred years before Alexander Hamilton wanted to rise up . . ."

In my bag, my phone vibrates. The buzz creeps against my ankle, insisting, urging. And it keeps going: quick, staccato stings that come one after the other. While Mr. Burkhart continues to outline chain steps in history, I lean over my bag.

Pretending to shuffle for some paper or a pencil or something, I turn the face of my phone toward me. Texts from Syd bubble up and float off the screen, so quick I almost miss them before I read them.

> I waited for you this morning and you never showed up.
>
> Then I saw you hanging out in the library.
>
> Since when are you friends with Hailey?
>
> Her dad's a cop btw. So don't let her see your ink.
>
> Seriously if she gets Amber shut down . . .
>
> I'll talk to you at lunch.
>
> ***Or will I?***

I drop the phone and sit back up, stung. We didn't plan to meet up this morning. I mean, we usually do. Her locker's close to mine, and we're best friends, and *obviously*. But it's not a law. We don't have a standing date.

Even if we did, *she* was the one who usually skipped it. She had boyfriend lockers to visit, girlfriend lockers to linger near—in random halls at random times on random days.

Instead of listening to Mr. Burkhart, I listened to Syd's voice in my head, saying the words from her text different ways. Variations on a theme: annoyed, worried, plaintive.

Which one is the right one? The venomous one that makes me feel like an enemy? Maybe the sarcastic one, where she's slightly irritated but annoyed at herself for being irritated?

The possibilities dig into my skin, burrowing under layers till they reach bone. My hands itch to answer. Why should Syd care if I'm friends with Hailey? Not that I *am* friends with her.

But Syd has a huge circle: people from work, people from classes I don't take, people from off the street and at the coffee shop and . . . basically, anywhere she goes. She collects people; I am one of many. (*First of many*, she likes to joke. Am I still?)

So that's weird, and the thread from *saw you talking to a classmate* to *we're maybe not speaking* is so knotted it makes no sense. I follow it again and again, and each time, I tangle it further. The more I think about it, the hotter my face gets. As I sit, spine pressed to the back of my seat, I feel my nose threatening to run.

Now my eyes are hot; my breath gets thin and my throat closes. That terrible, uncontrollable wobble ripples across my lower lip. I can't do this; I can't cry here. People already look at me—are they already looking at me?

I sit closest to the door, front row. It's the best angle to take notes from the overhead. Also, it means I can hit the hall right on the bell, before people surge to fill it. Strategic. Like the city of

Calais. For two hundred years, it was either England or France, just depending on the day.

I grab my bag, and pluck the bathroom pass off the wall. Mr. Burkhart has it attached to a fat Henry VIII doll that wheezes if you squeeze it. I do not squeeze.

I slink into the hallway, clammy and quiet. Instead of going to the closest bathroom to let the tears break, I slip down long corridors of medicinal green and industrial blue, far from history.

The air changes, from dry and papery to wet and earthy—welcome to the art department. I pass classrooms full of clay and chalk and charcoal, almost running now to the bathroom at the far back corner.

"Syd," I say, crashing into the door to open it.

Blue-silver hair pulled into a knot on the top of her head, Syd sits on the unused radiator beneath the windows. Ankles crossed, she tips her head when I burst in. She belongs here, down with the art; she's long limbs and angles, deep into her Blue Period.

Incredulous, she laughs. "What are you doing here?"

I shove my phone at her. "What's this?"

"Oh my god, I'm just messing around." She says it like she does stuff like this all the time; she doesn't.

My pulse sends messages in Morse code: SOS, Mayday, SOS. Everything tilts, like in a dream. The bad dream where I have to take a test and I'm late and running through molasses and when I finally get to class, I'm naked. So naked.

I say, "I'm sorry?"

For a moment, Syd closes her eyes. It's like she's gathering patience. To deal with *me*. Her best friend! Sliding to her feet, she slips an arm around me. Hugging me close to her side, she gives me a shake. It says, *We're so jolly; this is so okay*. Her mouth says, "I was just being stupid. I saw you with Hailey and I poked."

"It's not cool, Syd."

"*Sorry*," she says. The emphasis: I should accept things and move on. This alien moment; this pod Syd; this confrontational, bizarre stranger—accept them? Move on? Impossible.

"I just don't get it," I reply. "Why?"

Exasperated, Syd throws her arms up, peeling off me and walking to the sinks. She turns on a tap, thrusting her hands under the water as the sound fills the cold tile bathroom like white noise. "There's nothing to get. I was an idiot, okay? I got bored in econ and thought it would be funny. Obviously, I was wrong."

"Obviously," I say. It comes out too soft, too weak.

Long and graceful, Syd splashes her neck with delicate hands then cuts off the water. Two loose curls spring forward, making her perfect again. Plucking up her bag, she says, "I won't see you at lunch, though. That part was true. I have to make up a quiz in trig."

"Syd. Are you . . . mad at me or something?"

"God no, why?"

No reason, except for the bizarro texts, the tattoo she got without telling me, the breakup she executed without a murmur—and now we were both out of class. We don't miss class. So, on that note, why does she have something to make up in trig?

All those reasons sit on my tongue, weighing it down. She

already raised her voice, and I'm afraid if I say these things out loud, she'll laugh. Because I'm ridiculous. I sort of am ridiculous today.

"I don't know," I say finally. "It's been a weird day."

Sweeping close, Syd catches the back of my neck. She pulls me forward and dramatically *mwah*s a kiss on the crown of my head. "Go forth and have a better one. I love you. I'm sorry I toyed with your emotions."

I say, "It's okay."

And Syd, who knows everything about me, accepts that absolution and heads back to class.

FOR THE REST OF THE DAY, I WANT TO CRAWL OUT OF my skin.

As promised, Syd doesn't show during lunch. I eat alone, in one of the alcoves by the library. I fold myself small and pick at the bland Spicy Taco Bowl w/ Churro on a salmon-pink plastic tray. I'm not lonely there, just alone.

I could sit with Tenesta Jordan, if I wanted. We know each other from a polite distance. We've had lots of classes and a brief stint in the Girl Scouts together.

(I was in for about two months, before I got the scar.)

(I can't remember if I didn't want to go after that or if it was too weird to go.)

(Everybody knew.)

(Everybody was talking about it.)

When I think about it, there are a lot of people who would welcome me at their table. Isaiah Finch and I were #1 and #2 in Mr. Burkhart's History Bowl; Mariana Alonzo lives two houses down from me. Familiar faces speckle the cafeteria, bright anchor points welcoming me closer.

Any other day, I would ask to sit; they'd say yes. Conversation would be genial and food focused. *These taco bowls are terrible. Whatever this is, it isn't a churro. Look, I can squeeze the oil out of mine. Oh gross. Better than the Salisbury steak and splat of potatoes—amiright?* Forty minutes, tick-tick-tick and done.

But this particular day—snow in October, Syd in retrograde—demands deviation. I finish my lunch, alone. The rest of the day passes in textual silence.

When the last bell rings, I head for the parking lot. Syd drives, and she usually drops me off after school. But that was for usually. I haven't heard from her since we talked in the bathroom, and there's no way I can get on that bus. That teeming, screaming, groaning, overfilled bus, two to a seat and sometimes three. All in coats, all with bags.

Even now, people crowd the door. They look like goats, all trying to shove into the same spot at the same time. Bouncing and careening off each other, they bleat and growl and laugh.

My stomach turns, and I turn with it.

Across the student lot, I see Hailey digging for her keys at the side of a yellow VW Bug.

Frozen for a moment, I consider her and the way her long, black coat cuts just the right way. She's not a shapeless winter mass. She has shoulders, a waist, long legs that drip like honey into her boots.

The first bus pulls out, and I hurry across the barrier to get to her. I have to swallow against my dry tongue to revive it. When I do, I call out, "Hailey! Hey! Hey, Hailey!"

She straightens, one foot in the car, the other on frosty land. When she sees me, she smiles. "Hey! What's up?"

Already digging in my bag, I say, "If I gave you ten bucks for gas, could you take me downtown?"

Her smile turns curious. "Uh, for no bucks, I can give you a ride downtown."

"Are you sure?" I ask. "If it's too far out of your way . . ."

"I'm going to strength training down there," she says. "It's literally on my way."

The passenger door unlocks, and on the other side of the car, Hailey slides behind the steering wheel. She leans over to peer out the passenger window. "Coming?"

I hesitate. One last sweeping look across the parking lot. No Syd. No bus. Just me and a pretty girl smiling at me expectantly.

I get in.

HER CAR SMELLS LIKE ARMOR ALL AND FEBREZE, like cedar and citrus. The surfaces gleam—I read her fingerprints in the face of the stereo. This baby is new, at least to her. No McDonald's French fry has ever been left to petrify under these seats.

"Where to?" Hailey asks, merging into the line of cars trickling from the school.

"Corner of Broad and Main," I say. "Just going to go see a friend."

The scent of Febreze fades, the heater blasting out warmth and a sweet hint of Hailey's perfume. It stirs sparks across my skin. Safely buckled into a microcosm of her world, I steal a look at her. Everything about her sizzles in my cerebral cortex; she's sour lemon Pop Rocks on the tongue.

"Strength training, huh?" I say. "Like, lifting weights?"

Eyes firmly on the road, she nods. "Exactly. But not to get big. It's for stamina and strength. Soccer's a running game."

"You guys went to State last year, didn't you?"

Determination doesn't creep into her voice; it leaps, full-bodied and certain. "Yeah, and this year, we're gonna win it."

"Kill it and leave it on the floor," I say senselessly.

She laughs, and her laugh is wonderful. Kind of a low-rolling murmur that ends in a giggle for an exclamation point. Her details fascinate me, and I don't know why. Just, I've known her at a distance my whole life. I don't talk with her in libraries or ride with her in cars. I've never been alone with her until today.

Now, twice in one day.

It's not bad—like, I don't feel like I have to explain it to myself—it's just different. Hailey's really nice, and she likes Potter enough to have the hat and scarf, and a VW Bug is all in house colors.

All those things recommend her; it's just . . . it's unsettlement. (Not a word but a word now. And it describes what's going on with Syd, too: unsettlement. The opposite of our usual, steady, settled selves.)

I feel like Hailey and I talk on the way to Walker's Corner, but maybe not a lot? It seems like a long drive, though our school isn't really that far from downtown.

Everything in Maine twists around something else. Roads hug mountains and shorelines, piers huddle close to harbors, trees cling to river bends, and roads press close to all of them. Usually, I like that. Today, it makes me feel a little spun around. A little spun out.

I'm glad when Hailey turns onto the straight and narrow street that takes us into town.

Neither one of us gawks at the extremely cute brick facades. We've been here a thousand times, and we know all the brightness and baubles are for strangers. Inland Maine, working harder for those tourism dollars. We have to be kitschier and cuter, more pleasing to the eyes of antiquers everywhere.

By the time they get to us, they've already driven the coast on State Road One; they've already shopped through Bar Harbor and Broken Tooth and the Cranberry Islands. We have to be worth the trip.

The people who own the redbrick, up-and-down store faces on Main Street are currently making sure that everybody knows the Fall Color Festival is next week. (Though now it'll be somewhat muted because of the snow. *Maybe it will melt*, I imagine them hoping.) There are signs everywhere. People loooove small-town festivals.

"Where do you want me to drop you?" Hailey asks.

I point, as if she can see my ultimate destination. "If you turn past the candle store, there's a little drive that jogs close to the river. But if you don't want to go all the way back, you can drop me at the corner."

When she pulls up to the corner, she hesitates. I do too.

As I get out, she leans over the console. Her long hair, tawny and wavy, falls forward to frame her square face. It seems like she wants to say something, so I dip back in.

"You okay?" I ask.

"Yeah. Um . . . you're *sure* it's all right if I drop you here?"

I turn and it occurs to me just what she means. The wooded path. My . . . history.

The softness of Hailey's face, all gentle curves of lips and eyes, concerned and anxious—distracts me. She's kind and pretty, her gaze fixed on me.

My feet feel unsteady, and I clasp the roof of the car to catch my balance. All at once, I want to stay. Climb back in. Maybe I can watch some strength training. Maybe we can talk about *something*, have a real conversation. Wouldn't that be nice?

"Ava?"

I snap out of it. Hailey is a person I know at school. I made her slip out of her defined and designated circle by asking for a ride. I need to let her go, so she can fade behind the boundaries again. More emphatic than I intend, I say, "It's good, I'm good. Thanks again for the ride."

"If you're sure . . ."

Clapping a hand on the top of the car, I smile a smile I don't think I mean. "Totally. Thanks again."

Then I shut the door—not quick or hard, just final.

The walk to Amber's apartment *isn't* that far. It really isn't. The snow is mostly melted on the streets; I have a coat and both gloves; it's *fine.*

All of that comes from a rational voice that lives in my head, because it *has* to live in my head. It has to tell me what's safe and not safe, when to freak out and when to talk myself out of the freak-out. Sometimes that part of the brain seems broken.

But this is fine. Fine, fine, fine. The trees aren't that close to the road; there aren't that many of them. This is all town. It's urban(esque). It's not like *that* place, it's not.

Hailey was sweet and her car was warm and I'm sorry I'm not

in it anymore—but Syd is out there somewhere, silent. And if I stay any longer with Hailey, somehow it would feel like a betrayal.

Once again I have twisted into an uncomfortable knot; I know I can't loosen it on my own. Nothing makes sense, so I need clarity. Absolute clarity. My feet move fast, damp cold pressing against my sneakers.

As the converted warehouse comes into view, I settle. No voice needed anymore, because I know one thing for sure.

In just a minute, I'm going to feel better.

THE CHOICE IS A COMPROMISE BETWEEN THE financial and the temporal.

I can only get as much tattoo as I can afford and only as much ink as Amber can put in before I have to be home from school. My mother usually rolls in from work around six, so that gives me, at most, two hours in the chair and an hour to figure out how to get home.

Sorting through celebrity tattoos on my phone, I decide that two matching text pieces belonging to Harry Styles completely express how I feel at that moment. I show them to Amber, and she gets to work.

That doesn't mean firing up the equipment. It means drawing the two pieces, then tracing them onto some kind of transfer paper, then tracing them *again*. Amber lets me sit in the tattoo chair while she works. She makes conversation between pencil strokes.

"Been a while since you've been down here."

"Yeah, I had to go to my dad's for the summer."

"Sucks."

I shrug. "I saw the piece you did for Syd. It's sick."

"Thanks," she says. "It's a lot closer to the stuff I like to do on my own, so I had fun with it."

Amber's shoulders curve; she tapes down tracing paper and pulls out a thin black pen. Whenever she draws, she's all intensity. With brows furrowed, she presses her nose almost to the paper. The weight of art chains her to the table until she transfers it onto the stencil. Then, when she starts to tattoo, that weight seems to drift away.

If I were an artist, I think I'd get tired of drawing things for other people. What's the point in having all that talent if you can't use it to make yourself happy?

I ask her, "Do you wish you could just do what you want? Give someone whatever you thought suited them?"

"Sometimes."

"Does anybody ever let you?"

"Almost never."

I wonder about the outliers: the ones that make her say *almost*. What kind of person walks into a tattoo shop and says, "Give me what you think I need"? How endlessly brave would you have to be to let someone else leave their permanent opinion on your flesh? I rub my fingers along my scar, which itches.

For me, I know exactly what I want and I want to make sure it's coming out that way. I lean sideways in the chair, trying to catch a glimpse of the art as Amber cuts out the designs with a pair of tiny sharp scissors.

"Back up," she tells me. I do.

The tension, the good tension comes when she lays the stencils aside. It's time for her to wash and shave the inside of my arms, just above my elbow. They're tricky spots and hard places to try to hide.

But right at this moment—I don't know—I kind of don't care about any of that. Everybody else gets to leave a mark on me. Why can't I leave my own?

Amber rubs in lotion and presses the first stencil to the inside of my right arm. Familiar-unfamiliar smells wash over me. It's not my first tattoo, but Amber's soap isn't the soap I use at home. Lotion, I never use. Beneath the sheen, I see the stenciled letters tilt the right way: just what I asked for.

With a murmur under her breath, Amber snaps on latex gloves, then opens a fresh packet of needles.

I've watched her put the machine together so many times, but I'm always amazed that it all comes together in the end. This particular intersection of medical and industrial doesn't seem like it should work. Coils trail around the grip; tubes swirl out in long loops. It's a Frankenstein's monster of technology.

Finally, Amber turns it on. It works in spite of itself. The waspish buzz sends a tingle across my skin, every time.

"Don't move," she says, like I don't know better. Dipping the needle into black ink, she lifts her shoulders; she moves like she's floating.

A tattoo isn't one sting and then I get used to it. The sting goes on and on, making waves all the way to the tips of my toes. My face gets hot, sweat rising on my brow and my throat. It's like a flush without color; I just burn.

And inside the burn there's this blissful, empty place where everything smolders and all of my thoughts turn to embers lifted on the wind. Away and away, they all go away, and they leave a memory in black and grey on my skin.

By the time Amber finishes with me, both arms burn.

Turning out my right arm to admire it in the mirror, I smile. It says, **Things I Can**. The left doesn't match; it complements. It says, **Things I Can't**.

They're perfect, both of them perfect. I can't do anything about the weird skips of silence from Syd or the bright little comets of Hailey suddenly being *there*; all I can do is be a phoenix.

I rise from my own ashes.

I TRY TO RISE AND KEEP RISING—TRY TO PRETEND that everything is just the same as it was forty-eight hours before. That's to say, the way it was before Syd kept secrets from me and sent sharp texts tipped with poison (but not so, sayeth she). Before I sought out Hailey in the school parking lot.

I have to walk home. The closest Lyft is an hour away, in Presque Isle. If I wait, my mother will beat me home.

It's fine, all fine.

I cut down the path behind Amber's place, down to the river. It's actually a straighter shot to home than the road is. It's just going to take longer on foot in the snow. But it's better down here. Down where Walker's Corner is in the past, and the present is balsam and black ash and birch.

The sky darkens, dissolving into the pretty kind of twilight. Purples and blues; the darkness reveals the first stars, strung between the moon and the end of the universe. The trail by the water leads the way.

Other people's footsteps have already flattened the snow: proof that even this secluded place isn't deserted.

The woods stay on my right hand (*Things I Can*) and the river on the left (*Things I Can't*).

I've never been one of those people really impressed by the water. I mean, I get why people go to the beach. But even though I've got an anchor on my shoulder (Kacey Musgraves) and a sunset on waves on my thigh (Scarlett Johansson), I don't *get* it. Not the passion for the sea, for a river, for a lake, an ocean, a harbor.

There's a store up on Broad Street, for the tourists. It's full of lighthouse music boxes and *Lake House Girl* signs. Bumper stickers that say, "I'm not at home until I'm at the lake." Stained-glass window hangers full of seagulls and cliffs.

They're not for me. There's water *to* Maine and water *in* it; for me, that's about it.

But this path, with nature all around, is better than half-natural, half-industrial. I can breathe here. Cold air scours everything clean: my face, my lungs, my thoughts. The weight of my bag cuts into my shoulders. I test my theory that downtown isn't that far from home. It's all in the winding.

In case, though, just in case, I pull out my phone. Bars. I text Syd with the first thing that comes to mind. Amber said your last tat is probably her favorite ever.

I do that sometimes. Exaggerate. Massage the truth. Lie—

(Just, I want you to know, I'm not doing it *now*. I'm being really specific with *you* about when I tell the truth and when I don't.) (I try to be an honest liar.) So yeah, Syd rewards me with a quick reply. Quick, like texts are supposed to be: Shut up.

She says it's like the stuff she'd do on her own, I reply. Because that was the truth for real, and therefore, if Syd ever mentions it to Amber, the sliding edges around the first statement would feel like a game of Telephone.

With the reply of the turkey emoji, Syd says everything and nothing.

(Why does she say nothing? I went to Amber's without *her. I got inked* without *her; I have new ink and she doesn't even ask what I got; she doesn't care. She's not jealousangrypossessiveanything.)*

Instead, she asks, How did you get there?

Caught a ride with Hailey. Did you wait for me? I ask.

Obviously.

I thought you were busy.

Guess you don't get paid for thinking.

I stop short. The cold presses down, the clouds a low silver ceiling that promises more snow, soon. The river whispers; the trees shush it, and a storm slowly grows in my head. Not curiosity; accusation. I can't tell if I'm angry or upset as I thumb back, Seriously, are you mad at me?

I'm not mad! omfg!

I take a sharp half breath, then sit on a fallen tree. Cold presses through my coat, through my pants, uncomfortable but present.

The last thing I need is to get in a fight with my best friend and accidentally walk into the river. It would become a tragedy of lies: people talking about how I never *seemed* depressed, they all missed the warning signs, my mother shocked and broken because she didn't see it coming.

(Supposition and exposition and embroidery all over again.

Did you hear about the girl with the scar? Yeah, she offed herself. I guess she never got over it. Should we do something? Let's do candles and a GoFundMe for suicide stuff or . . . the other thing. You know, ***the other thing.***)

It's been a really long day, I start, then hesitate. On Syd's side, she just sees •••.

•••, she non-replies.

I don't understand why we're fighting. I don't understand why I'm apologizing. I sit, poised to reply, and my arms protest. Both sides, the layers of T-shirt and sweater and coat bunch up, grinding knots into my new ink. The sting burns deeper, and I realize I already know what to do with this screwed-up situation. Since I can't fix it and everything I say makes it worse, well . . .

THINGS I CAN'T.

That's what I file it under. I delete my unsent wibbling, then shove my phone in my pocket. For a minute, I sit there and breathe. It's me and the vapor of my breath hanging in the air. The dark creeps up fast, rolling off the river like smoke. It chases me from the log and into ascent, through the thick trees, up the steep hill.

It would have been hard to climb this on a summer's day.

On a wintery autumn's evening, each hidden root and crevice are part of the monster under the bed, grasping at your ankles and catching your toes until you jump to the safety of your pillows and sheets.

A bright hot pain spikes through my ankle. I twist; I fall.

Snow plumes around me. Sinking into my gloves, the wet chill climbs faster than I did. Even though I shove myself up and keep moving, it reaches my skin before I'm halfway to the road above. The trees crowd over me like they're watching a fight. In a way, I guess they are. Ava versus Nature, Ava versus Herself.

I berate myself as I struggle for another six inches, a foot. I'm the stupidest. I should have followedthehighwaycalledanUbertext-edmymomgrabbedadifferenttree—

It's not a tree; it's a log, bare of snow.

It looks like a good handhold, but it cracks when I grab it. The sound whips over my head, echoing into the coming night. Dank wood crashes into me. Flailing, falling, I taste iron, blood—

Am I bleeding? Did I hit the ground?

The log rolls past me, a few more heavy thumps before it comes to rest. Out of reflex, I drag a hand down my face. Snow grinds into my skin like glass, but no red bleeds onto my gloves. The blood—I imagined it? Hallucinated it?

Awkward, I struggle to sit up. And when I do, I see her face. Her grey, shattered face.

And her naked body, stuffed into the other half of the tree.

THIS IS WHERE I MAKE A DECISION AND YOU'RE going to think, *Oh, because.*

And this time, you'll be right. But you'll be wrong, too. So many things flow into and swirl around *because* that there's no way to separate the elements afterward.

I sit in the snow, staring at this girl for hours or maybe seconds. Her body isn't like a TV corpse, smooth and beautiful.

V-shaped gouges on her chest reveal jelly layers of pink and grey and yellow; her body splays in a chaotic sprawl.

She's twisted like a Barbie doll at the waist. Her top half points forward, baring her face, her chest, those Vs. It takes me a minute to realize that they're stab wounds. Her bottom half faces down. Somehow both her breasts and her butt are exposed at the same time.

(she has a tattoo)

Human people, alive people, they don't make that shape.

(she has a tattoo, a symbol, I know it—astrology, Aquarius, I think)

With toes dug into the ground and her arms—god, where are

her arms? I can't find her arms—and her everything, she looks like she's been tossed carelessly into a box.

Purple outlines the cheek that rests against the ground. Lips swollen, eyelids swollen. She's a reflection in a fun house mirror, pulled from the glass.

I don't know where the smell of blood is coming from; I don't want to. Rising on my knees, I slap at my pockets. Phone, phone, I have a phone. Where's my phone; I lost my phone, where is my phone?!

Afraid, I don't look away from her. If I blink and she disappears, I'm losing my mind. If I blink and she doesn't, then I've disturbed an unmarked grave. On a hill. In a wood. By a river. Where I didn't belong. Where maybe I am not *alone.*

I mutter, and my words fog the air with each breath, each pocket slap. "Come on, come on, come on."

I bite the fingers of my gloves, then pull them off. I have to find my phone, have to call the police and call my mom and call the police and . . . finally. My pocket has a hole in it; my phone slipped into the shell of my coat. When I finally fish it out, my coat's lining tears with a sickening rip.

The girl doesn't stare at me. Not because her eyes aren't open; they are. But there's a bloody black line where the whites should be; I can't make out her iris or pupils. This makes her silence a special kind of still, unnerving and ominous. All those things people say at a funeral (*she looks so peaceful, she looks just like she's asleep*) aren't true. Not here. She's

(been violated)

miserably empty. She's

(cut deep but no scar, she's never going to have a scar, a scar is something that healed)

dead.

Just dead.

Fumbling to dial—anger, humiliation, fear—and god, I know what comes next. When I push that panic button, when I call 911, the sirens will come.

Men, probably men, with heavy shoes and heavy belts will tower over the spectacle. Looking past this girl's body, the young cop will key the mic on his shoulder and say, "Yeah, dispatch, we've got remains down here. Caucasian female, late teens, early twenties."

Around and around her body they'll circle, ravens looking for scraps. They won't touch her. Neither will the detectives, although they might poke her with the end of a pen to see if there's anything under her. They might chat. Heat ghosts will trail off their cups of coffee; they'll talk about the weather. As though she isn't *right there* beneath them.

The pop and whine of a flash will fill the scene. A strobe light for a murder rave, zooming in on her bare skin and her wounds and her vulnerability—the camera never blinks.

Here comes the coroner; she'll touch. She'll get a couple guys to help her roll the body. On her count—one, two three—onto a flattened gurney, into a black body bag.

That won't be the end.

That's not the end—because there's *always* a *what happens next* when bodies are violatedabusedassaultedmolested. In the medical examiner's office, this girl probably won't be shoved into stirrups (like I was), but they will take samples.

S A M P L E S, from her mouth, from her vagina, from her anus . . . If the coroner finds any saddle-shaped bruises, bite marks!—swabs for those, too. More pictures and an audio guide narrated by a woman with a scalpel.

She'll take this girl apart, she'll open her skin, she'll open her head, her chest, she'll dig out everything that was ever *her* and weigh it.

The pictures could end up on the internet (people like crime scene photos).

Her body would belong to everyone and not her, forever and ever, amen.

And all this will happen, whether they find the person who did this or not.

It will probably be *not.*

(Mine was not. He's still out there, that curly-haired man. . . .)

So the cops, the coroner, they'll do all that to her. They will empty her out for . . . *nothing.*

My stomach clenches, and that sour spring of spit rises in my throat. I hold my phone in dead hands, my thumbs frozen over the screen. Nine-one-one refuses to form beneath my touch. I open my Favorites and look at my mom's avatar. She wears a pink feather boa and a silver crown; it's a picture from her birthday last year. All I have to do is touch her to summon her.

I want her. I want my mom to make everything better. That's

her job, right? She's supposed to make everything better.

And I don't know why I believe that. I know the truth.

I wear the proof on my face—evidence that she can't make *everything* better.

Being real with you—I don't think she can make *anything* better.

When Syd's mom encourages her to go to school dances that she doesn't want to go to, my mother says, "Let's get a Redbox and make popcorn."

Pep rallies and extracurriculars? How about an avocado mask and a spa night instead? My mom never pushes. She stands sentinel and lets me lock myself away. She builds a pleasant tower, and cuts my hair so it doesn't grow long enough to fall to the ground. Does she do it because I want it? Because she needs it?

She must have known all along.

Every time I leave my cage, something terrible happens. Sometimes it's the worst thing; sometimes it's just a bad thing.

Sometimes it's a body in the woods.

Sitting there in the woods, full of fear that wraps around my heart and lungs, I realize two things.

I am alone.

I have *always* been alone.

And I alone know what happens next, to this girl. How much more she has to endure. How much less she'll become. How public they'll make her flesh.

What do I do?

What am I going to do?

ONE need not be a chamber to be haunted,
One need not be a house;
The brain has corridors surpassing
Material place.

—EMILY DICKINSON,
Part Four: Time and Eternity; LXIX

I GO HOME; I TAKE A SHOWER.

After, when I'm scalded red and there's no hot water left, I put on underwear, a cami, a T-shirt, and the sweat suit I kept from freshman gym. It's dark green, with an Aroostook North Woodman

(Go, Fightin' Lumberjacks!)

embroidered on the hoodie. Then a hat: a knit hat that holds the humidity in my hair.

At my desk, I use a stapler to fix the lining of my coat. If we ever had needles and thread, I don't know where to find them. We're not handy like that, my mom and me. When the stitching pops on her favorite comforter, Mom takes it to the cleaner. They wash it, repair it, package it up nice and neat.

So I use a stapler. It does the trick. After that, homework. Mom comes in while I'm reading about the Antonine Plague. Yes, I beat her home. Beat her by a mile.

Up the hill, onto the main road, I booked it, and it was maybe fifteen, twenty more minutes?

My mother calls me down to dinner, and I leave the stapler and coat on my desk. The insides of my arms burn, my new tattoos like brands beneath my sleeves. I hold ***Things I Can't*** against my waist, clutching the stair rail with ***Things I Can***.

"How was school?" Mom asks, unpacking a stack of lo mein and General Tso's from Mrs. Lin's. The spicy sweetness of the General Tso's is like a spike up my nose. Usually, I love it, but right now it's too much. I put it aside and sniff the other cartons until I find plain, steamed rice. "It was school, you know."

"Mm," Mom says, distracted. She turns around, three halting loops before she finds what she lost: the fork that was already sitting on the table, next to her lo mein. "Homework?"

Tucking myself into a chair, I pop the top of the steamed rice and dose it with soy sauce. "Almost done."

Everything is normal. So normal. She sits down, then pops back up to get a paper towel to use as a napkin. She spills her dinner onto a plate. Unashamed that she never learned to use chopsticks, she digs into her plate with a fork and gusto.

Her eyes rise, skimming my face. She's conversational. She says, "It's supposed to snow again tonight."

I know. I don't say that because when do I ever look at the weather? Except tonight, on my phone—after the shower, before the stapler. Snow and snow, huge accumulations.

There will be a fresh, new white blanket on the ground in the morning. It will be pristine and untouched. It will cover up all the dark things left on the ground, splayed on the earth. All will be tucked in tight, temperatures below freezing—

"I thought I saw your car off the side of the road," I say. "On the way to school."

"Oh, honey," Mom says. Her voice is warm; it melts her and softens her expression. She reaches over and rubs my shoulder. "I'm fine. You don't need to worry about me."

"It's everybody else I worry about," I say.

All the other drivers in the world, all the other best friends in the world, all the other pretty Hufflepuffs in the world—

Mom swishes her fork through her noodles. "It's all right, Ava. It happens every year."

It just feels strange and hollow to hear that, because it's true. It happens every year.

Things happen every year.

Important things.

Something important *happened*. Today. In the woods. It's *still* happening.

And my mother can't even tell.

I FORGOT TO CLOSE MY CURTAINS BEFORE I WENT TO bed.

When I wake up at 3:32 a.m., I roll over to see snow falling beyond the dark glass. It comes down in fluffy, cotton ball puffs. They're too fat to swirl, but the wind shifts them as they fall. An angle to the left, an angle to the right, they flicker like pixels.

On the bedside table, my phone vibrates, its facedown screen suddenly glowing. That was what woke me up, had to be.

I don't want to unfold and stretch an arm outside the covers. I'm lying in the perfect position. I'm so exquisitely comfortable, I feel like an ancient queen arrayed for beauty and power. I have those moments, sometimes. Where I'm so possessed in my body that I almost feel like a god. It never lasts more than a moment.

The phone vibrates again. Now I reach for it.

I was a bitch before.

I'm ovulating and I have a big-ass cyst and it hurts.

Anyway yeah. hmu if you want a ride in the morning.

Syd's voice is in my head now. I let it press at the tender spots, the ones she left earlier with jabs and claws and confusion. There's still an ache there, but the spot that wants everything to be normal and okay is bigger. It wraps around her words and turns them into an apology, one that I accept.

NBD, I tell her. No big deal. A lie like her apology: forgiveness that isn't but is. It's snowing again and I'm out of the way.

So? she says. It's a statement with a question mark.

Okay, see you in . . . I look at the clock on my phone. Ugh, 3 hours.

kk.

Now silence, for so long the screen dims. From the corner of my eye, I see motion. It's just snow, I'm sure of it, but I look just in case. And there, in my window is her face.

Her face.

She shouldn't be up this high. My bedroom sits at the top of a long staircase. The house is old; the stairs are steep. There's no trellis or porch or tree to climb; she shouldn't be up this high. Panic constricts my heart. It beats in a strange, too-long pattern that almost feels like holding my breath.

Suggestions of her eyes, her lips, they flicker in the glass. She looks in but past me. Like she's waiting for something in the distance, just beyond my bed. When she digs all five fingers into her hair, I count the rings she wears: one, two, three. They're pale and cheap; so is her jean jacket.

I know (I know, I *know*) that she (herbody) isn't here. That was bare, and I pulled the log back up to cover her. I made sure she was covered, she was safe. With raw hands, I pushed snow up against all the cracks and crevices, a mortar to seal her in. It's not just cold outside. It's frigid, and this fat, wet snow will keep her.

She's safe.

She's with me.

Her gaze travels from the middle distance to fall on me. She's an impressionist painting; I can't make out her details. But I do see her smile. It's crooked and knowing. It only reaches one eye. It speaks to me directly.

We have a secret, don't we?

IN THE MORNING, SYD SHOWS UP in her stepfather's Jeep Grand Cherokee. The thing is huge inside—black, with black leather seats, satellite radio, and a back-up camera. Straining to open the passenger door, she explains before I even ask. "He thought it would be safer."

It feels it. High off the ground, headlamps bright as searchlights, broad. Sturdy. And even though I quietly judge people in SUVs, I hope that this monster *is* safer.

Overnight, we got another eight inches. Even where they're plowed, the roads are mushy and indistinct. I like the way they seem carved out of the earth, but I don't like the way they build secret ice beneath the snow. *Where's the Black Ice?* A game nobody wants to play.

Pulling on my seat belt, I tell her, "He's turning out to be a nice guy, huh?"

"I reserve the right to withhold judgment," she says.

Fair enough. Skip isn't her first stepfather. He's not even her second. Maybe he's still in that honeymoon phase, showing off for his new wife. *Look how great I am, check out this manly, manly provider routine!*

Also, his name is Stephen, but he wants people—including me—to call him Skip. Anybody who shortens themselves to a dog's name is automatically suspect. I pointed this out to Syd; she agreed. She practically embroidered it on a throw pillow.

Syd throws the behemoth into gear, and I open Neko Atsume on my phone. It's a pointless game, but I love it. I have to check on my tiny kitties, to see what presents they brought in the night. I earn coins to buy cuter cat toys to attract more cats so they'll bring me more presents. Like I said, pointless. But cute.

My phone fills the cab with a low glow, and Syd glances over.

"Anything good?"

"One of them brought me birthday candles."

Cheerfully, Syd turns onto the main road. "Thanks, mau mau kitty."

As I sort my digital cats and buy them digital toys, I settle beside Syd. I settle, but I don't relax. I'm waiting for her to look over and see this secret written into my skin. To know what I'm not telling her; to see that face in the snow, eyes unclosed forever. My face flushes. My scar feels red and hot. Glowing—a beacon.

Syd turns on the radio, then talks over it. "I'm not trying to make you mad—"

"Never a good start," I interrupt.

"I just want to know what the deal is with Hailey."

My god. She's actually wound up about this. Syd's proud face is a little softer this morning. Her voice is, too. It's a statement but not a demand.

I buy my cats a macaron pillow to sleep on. Cute kitties sleeping on cute cookies. Is there no end to the high-grade kawaii I can mainline with this game? Rubbing my lips together, I say, "There's no deal, Syd. I dropped my glove, and she gave it back to me."

"And she drove you home."

"No, she drove me into town, which I told you." I'm nitpicking, but it's all in the details. "I walked home."

Shocked, Syd exclaims, "What the what?!"

"It's really not that far," I say, rearranging furniture so more cats will visit me. Nothing bad happens in Neko Atsume. Even when the cats bring something dead, like a cicada skin, it's in the most adorable fashion possible.

At the stoplight, Syd drapes her wrists over the wheel. "It's far."

"It's really not that far," I repeat.

All around us, the snow glows red from taillights. People are slower this morning. They edge through intersections and start braking a quarter mile away, at least. With the heater on full blast, our windows in the Jeep are bright and clear. Our breath doesn't fog in the air. But I can feel the cold from the outside pushing in.

Wriggling her gloved fingers, Syd takes the wheel again when the light changes. "You went to town. You got a tattoo?"

"Two," I say.

The tires make a soft kissing sound. The road whisks as the wheels cut through slush. We feel solid and safe; Syd drives slower than usual, but I think that's because it's Skip's car, not because of the weather. Every so often, we'll cut a curve and the kiss turns to a groan—tires compressing new snow.

(She's out there, under new snow. She's safe there.)

"Well?" Syd says.

I turn my phone facedown. The cab goes dark. Underneath the radio playing Top 40, the jingly, jaunty music of Neko Atsume tootles on. *(What a small, strange, leather-clad circus this is.)* I raise an arm. Syd can't see through my coat, but it gives her an idea where the words sting under layers of wool and polyester and Tegaderm.

"'Things I Can't,'" I say. Then the other arm. "'Things I Can.'"

Syd frowns, her face bathed in the red glow of taillights. "Whose are they?"

"Harry Styles."

"Oh."

Then quiet. Not silence; there's too much music, too much traffic and weather, to call this silence. It's a voicelessness that has its own waver to it. It's a space to fill with assumptions, which I do. I say, "I didn't think you'd care; you got your beehives without me."

"You weren't here when I got the outline, though," Syd points out. "If you'd been here . . ."

"I'm sorry," I say. I mean it. Again, it's assumptions, but with some people, you can make them. You know them well enough to think for them and call back to them before they speak. She's been my best (only) friend for so long, it *is* a little weird for me to talk to someone else, get a ride from someone else, potentially get ink with someone else.

It probably felt to her like I was shopping for replacement parts, auditioning for the role of best friend—the new girl! I can see how it looks if I stand there in her embroidered boots and pastel curls.

"I don't want you to be sorry," Syd says; she means it. There's guilt in there now, for feeling insecure, for taking it out on me.

With a nod, I accept an apology she didn't give.

"I really don't. I mean, Hailey's nice. If you want to hang out with her, you should. We could even hang out together."

That pulls a thread, a curling, twisting thread that's supposed to hold my stomach in place. My everything shifts, misplacing my insides. Uncomfortable, I say, "Yeah, maybe."

"Cool."

Mollified, Syd drums her fingers on the wheel again. I lay my temple against the window and look into the woods. In this light, there's the black insinuation of trees and white snow. *Was it this curve?* I wonder. *This curve on the road where I came up from the river? Was it that rock there? Are my footprints buried here?*

I exhale heavily, my breath steaming the glass. The heat in the car wipes it away, and there, with arms stretched between two forks of a tree, my secret girl stands. The wind pulls her hair; the silver stud buttons on her jacket flicker as cars pass. Twisting, I turn to watch her until we cruise around the bend.

If she's going to haunt me, she needs a name.

I DIDN'T REALIZE HOW OFTEN MY SCHEDULE LINED up with Hailey's until today. Between first and second block, and again between second and third, I smile and she waves.

When I stream into the caf with the rest of B Lunch, my gaze falls on her instantly. She cradles a GladWare bowl to her chest, and she's turned on the bench and talking to (pretty sure it's) Avery Grace (could be her twin sister, Harper).

With my turkey sandwich in hand, I stand beside one of the pillars and watch Hailey. Her fingers skim through her hair, sweeping it behind one ear. A gold earring climbs the shell, a design I can't make out. All I know is that it glitters when she moves, and she moves so much when she talks.

Every part of her lives: light in her eyes, music in her fingertips. When Avery/Harper backs away, Hailey smiles a goodbye. She waits till Harper/Avery turns away to go back to her lunch.

Except her amber eyes play across the faces around her, then land on me. There's a spark under my skin; it feels like a fire trying to start.

I push off the pillar and take the long walk across the caf. My face is warm, the kindling inside me starting to catch. My feet glide, and I reach Hailey without taking a step. That's what it feels like; that's really what it feels like.

"Hey," she says, sliding over.

Accepting that invitation, I sit beside her. "Hey!"

Too loud? Too excited for a hello? I can't tell. The plastic on my sandwich crinkles between my hands; why am I smashing it instead of opening it? "Thanks again for the ride yesterday."

Her smile is warm and round, and she shrugs. She tips her bag of mini chocolate-chip cookies toward me. "I was happy to help. Anytime."

Somehow I laugh. I *tease*. "You probably shouldn't feed strays." I take a cookie anyway.

When she looks down, then up at me again, the hair she smoothed back falls against her cheek. "I'm a fan of rescues, actually."

Ignition. The spark finally catches, and my whole body goes hot. Too hot. My face feels sweaty; my hands stick to the wrapper on my sandwich. I'm not sure what to say, so I pivot awkwardly. "So, strength training. How was it?"

"I love it, like, so much." She forks up a bite from her bowl. "It makes me feel so good. If you ever want to try . . ."

She lets the silence ask the question. And even though the caf roars with starving juniors, I hear Hailey's breath over all of it. I hear the click of her fork against plastic; it's like knowing someone in the school chorus. No matter the song, no matter the show, I can always hear Syd over the rest.

Finally, I say, "Do you have, like, tiny baby barbells?"

"The tiniest," she says with a laugh. Fingers in her hair, swoop again. The gold that decorates her ear is a series of climbing leaves. They climb the curve, reach the peak, curl against her skin possessively. "We have infants in class, you know. They bring weighted rattles."

"I'm going to bring two of these," I say. And a possessed demon spirit inside me tosses my sandwich in the air gently, and thank god, my hand catches it. What is wrong with me?

Hailey's smile spreads. "Protein is important."

I don't know what to say next, and I don't know why. I'm not usually bad at making conversation. But I'm sitting beside and not across. Hailey's elbow brushes mine, and it's not bad. It's an unexpected touch, but it doesn't make me want to jerk away.

Since I let my end of the conversation drop, Hailey picks it up. Not seamlessly but with effort. "I'm glad you came over. I was worried about you getting home okay."

She worried about me. She sat in her room, in her house, with her parents downstairs and she thought about *me*. I was in her mind, alive and present.

That means she was there, with me, walking along the river—in the glow of the sunset, in the cold of the snow.

She was with me when I climbed, when I fell.

When I found *her*.

(I still don't have a name. Jane? Maybe too generic. Did she look

like a Lauren? A Taylor? Maybe a Hannah?)

(She looks like a dead girl—

There's snow falling on her right now and . . .)

Not that. Not that thought. I push it down hard. "I walked. Didn't plan that very well, did I?"

"Oh my god, no," Hailey says, and she catches my arm. My bicep, below my shoulder, above my elbow. "You should have called me. I mean, how long did that take? I could have driven you home."

"I didn't want to bother you."

"Bother me," she says as her grip softens. Now it's more like she's just resting her hand against me. "I don't mind. Seriously."

All of a sudden, I feel out of my body. Not in a bad way, exactly. More like I'm there but not quite there; taking up space and no space at all. I hear myself talking, but I don't feel it. I witness it.

Fortunately, the thing that keeps my body moving and my mouth speaking doesn't embarrass me. "I will. Next time, I'll bother you. Maybe I'll bother you even if I don't need anything—bother you just for fun."

Hailey's fingers curl on my arm. As they slip away, her nails catch on the loops of my sweater. It's like the strum of guitar strings, the vibration transmitted directly to my spine. It pulls me back into place, so I feel the shock of what she says next. "Good."

The half bell rings; we both look at the ceiling, accusing it of interruption. Hailey takes two tries to screw the lid back on her lunch bowl, and she shoves the whole thing into her backpack. Half standing, she slings her bag over her shoulder. "Time for trig, lucky me."

"I'll catch you later." And then I say, "See? Strays. You never get rid of them."

Her smile burns everything away.

YES, I AM DOING THINGS. I'M GOING TO CLASS, TO lunch, to the media center. I'm checking my tattoos because they burn a little and need more lube. I ate my dinner. I ate my lunch. I'm probably going to buck for pizza again tonight. I am getting by.

How to Get By, a quick guide, by me.

The key factor in getting by is boxes.

So many boxes. Compartments of varying security where each thing goes.

Happy memories only need boxes if they're the kind that turn bittersweet. The smell of fennel and star anise in your grandmother's kitchen, floating up with onion and garlic in olive oil. So good. Until grandma passes away, and then the scent takes you back in time to a place that doesn't exist in the present.

I wouldn't say you avoid this box. The lid can stay on loosely; it just needs to be set aside so you can survive Italian restaurants without breaking down.

Boxes for the bad things—you're gonna need a lot of them. The stupid things you said two years ago to somebody you just met: those need to be packed away in boxes with sealable lids. The memories still get out sometimes, late at night, but otherwise, they suffocate in the dark, unexamined.

Fights you had with your father when he moved out one day and left your mother to explain where he went. Leave that box open. That way, when he does something else inexcusable, like calling the day *after* your birthday or asking what grade you're in again, the box is ready with all your grievances. They stay fresh this way, and if you give them enough air, they grow like sourdough.

Some boxes are mysterious. You don't label them at the time, and now they're full of vaguely familiar dust. What was it that you said that made Uncle Leonard so mad? Why don't you eat green bean casserole anymore? There are REASONS, but they're lost.

The things in some boxes beat against the walls to be let out. The man who once promised me something that felt good in the summer lives in a box like this. There are lies in there and also the big ugly truth.

It thrashes around. Sometimes it explodes, and shrapnel buries deep in your heart and your bones, and you have to pick out every single piece before you can put it back.

Boxes like that—with things that you know but deny about yourself—those boxes rattle all around. They threaten, like hand grenades.

Maybe they need tape or staples or chains. But you have to keep them closed, or they'll explode and kill you.

One of my boxes is now a hollowed-out tree heaped with snow.

So what do you do with a box like that? You tell yourself you can't see it. Can't see it; it's not there. Look past it; admire the scenery all around it. Check out all those trees, happy little trees. And the memory of the box recedes into some fold in the corner of your brain. This is good. This is fine. This is the way things should be.

This is the way all the boxes should be, really. Closed up, stacked, manageable, and managed. Beneath notice, inert. That's how you get by: you live in the present and you do NOT look back at the rows and rows of memories. Don't look. Just keep going.

Keep moving. Don't ever stop.

Things I can. Things I can't.

This is how I get by.

I'M CAREFUL TO TEXT SYD, TO EXPLICITLY TELL HER that I am on the bus.

She replies with a perfectly curated wtf? that I ignore. I worry the phone in my hands, ignoring Syd and wishing I could text Hailey. Too bad for me; I was too busy throwing stupid sandwiches to ask for her number.

Now, I could figure out her email address. The school gives them to us—*lastname-firstinitial@aroostook.k12.me.us*—but it would be weird to write her. That's seriously a step up. Email is bigger than text; I will not email her.

I listen for the last bus to leave; the cars are next. Then I slip out of school and tighten my hood. I need to think about geography: the nearest curve of the river, how far that is from town, and which bend is the right bend.

I open Maps on my phone and figure I'll see just how long my signal holds. The woods line the back of the track. By heading across it, toward them, I'm pointed right for the river.

Thick trees pull at my coat, and a heavy pack of snow tugs at my boots. This is a crazystupiddangerous thing to do, but I have to. She's out there alone, and I need to make sure she's okay.

(I think I'll call her Jane; it's a name that melts to nothingness.)

Jane Pending, Jane Until. Until what, I don't know.

I do know that seeing her last night, through the dark and on the other side of my bedroom window, means that she's *with me.* She trusts me not to betray her.

I won't tell anyone about her. She's a secret, locked up tight.

I know her, at least a little. I know her fear in her almost last moments.

I bet she wouldn't even ask me about the scar. She'd sit next to me on a fallen tree, and we'd look at the water and not talk about that *thing* they did to us at all, both knowing what we know, sharing what we share.

This all makes me laugh, a little, with running nose and wet gloves, as I slog through the trees to the riverbank. Syd's acting like a nervous cat because I'm talking to Hailey. She would lose it completely if she knew about Jane. I mean, all I got from Hailey is a ride. Jane's got my secrets cut into her flesh.

Following the river backward, I feel like I'm unpeeling time. The water's current moves in the wrong direction. The sun creeps ever lower behind my back, like it's trying to sneak into the horizon. No wind scours my face today. Instead, it pushes me along. *walk faster, walk faster*, it says.

And it's a good thing I do.

I recognize my landmarks and turn to look up the hill where Jane lies, closed up in her tree like the heart of a secret.

I would go to her, but I can't.

Someone's there.

A BOY IS THERE.

He's standing thereTHERETHERE where her eyes are open but her body is covered and protected and safe and he'd have to KNOW what's there to stand there, he'd have to KNOW.

Time slows down. I feel the pull and push of my own ragged breath. I take in so many details, not even on purpose. But I see him, and it's like bullet time, the world an anchor point that I revolve around. His skin is pale, stark white against his black coat, like snow spilled into the wool to make his shape.

He shivers; he chews his full lips. His thick brows dig deep into his forehead. He stands over Jane's quiet place; he just stands there. Hands in pockets, head hung low. He's at a funeral, at her funeral.

A funeral he must have planned, because otherwise, how would he know where to stand? I found her by accident, and there's no sign of her on the brand-new snow. There's a shapely curve in the white; a nearby stump stands like a headstone.

Some of the trees are broken, the branches, the lowest branches, and that's where, I think, I ran back up to the road yesterday. I'm numb, staring, watching him. I float until he frees a hand and reaches down.

"Hey!" I yell.

His head snaps up. The hood of his coat falls back. More details. Wavy blond hair, short on the sides. Cut neat around his ears and against the nape of his neck. His eyes widen.

Two eternal seconds and we both stand in place, staring at each other.

Then he runs.

"Stop!" My cry cracks the air like gunshot as I bolt after him.

Cutting up through the trees, he doesn't look back—grabs branches for balance and scuttles up the ridge. He leaves a deep furrow for me to follow, but it's like running in a dream. Everything is slow, and fighting harder makes me slower.

He gets farther away, six steps for three of mine. I will catch him. I have to; I have to hold him down. Make him answer; make him pay.

My blood runs faster, hotter in my veins. The heat loosens me up, and my mouth is wet. It's like my teeth are sharper. It's a hunt, and my body doesn't understand that only bad people chase prey in the twenty-first century.

Except he *is* my prey. Because of what he did. What he must have done. *(Like what he did to me. Not him but someone like him. Just like him.)*

I want to hit him. I want to hurt him.

When I scream this time, it feels like something breaks in my throat. "Stop!"

Instead, he runs faster. He's sleek and swift, and starting to blend into the trees.

I put my head down and try to cut the distance between us. A thousand pinprick sunrises sting my cheeks; it feels like every capillary has burst. My ears are full of drums, and my gut is knotted tight. I have to catch him, and when I catch him, I'm going to

(eat him all up)

(my, what big eyes you have...)

I don't know what I'm going to do, and that single, distracting thought steals my balance. The roots and brambles beneath the pines catch my ankles and I fall, again. Just like before, because the forest is dark and deep and its dangers never change.

I scrabble back to my feet, but two more steps and I fall again. Tears of frustration spill over. I push up on all fours. I don't try to stand.

The crush of his feet, the sound of his jeans rasping as he runs, all fade away. He's gone. I slump and roll onto my back. Above me, the thick pines and tangled, skeletal birches make a strange canopy.

Shaking all over, I rake a snow-caked hand beneath my nose to stop the running. I choose my next breath, drawing it deep and hard until my lungs ache with it.

That boy. He hurt

(murdered)

my Jane,

and I let him get away.

I'm not strong. I'm not fleet. I'm not a predator. I'm just an idiot rabbit who didn't think about what would happen if she caught the wolf.

WITH MY TEETH, I PULL OFF MY GLOVES AS I WALK into town. Town is full of kitsch, but it's also full of boutique coffee shops and warm places. I need warm. My hands are so cold, my phone barely recognizes my touch. I'm lucky that autocorrect keeps a record of my consistency.

Knock knock Syd. Now you say who's there.

She replies, Who's there?

Banana.

There's a pause, and then she texts back, Lol don't start with me, heifer. What were you doing on the bus?

Getting a ride, duh. Are you busy right now?

Yeah, kinda. What's up?

I could tell her. *Could I tell her?* If I did, she'd help me find the guy who got away. We'd drive around in her stepdad's Jeep, treating it like the Mystery Machine. Syd and Ava's Hardcore Detective Agency. We solve murders with style.

Light glances across the screen of my phone, and I see Jane reflected there. She makes this knowing, amused face as she shakes her head.

No.

She means, *No, you can't tell. Not Syd, not anybody.*

It's personal and confidential. Our friendship belongs in a sacred vault, and it needs to stay there. The chasm between the real world and our relationship is too wide. Too sharp, too dangerous.

All of a sudden, I want to cry. Jane's out there in the woods, all alone. It's cold and it's dark, and I'm not the only one who knows where she is. What was he going to do, when he reached for her? Was he going to touch her again? Was he—

I stuff that box down, fast and hard. Some things, I don't need to think. I don't need to ever, ever think. I cross the bridge into town, and rub my fingers against my jeans to warm them.

You there? Syd asks.

Yeah. I let autocorrect tell Syd, Sorry. Just bored.

K, talk later. Remind me to tell you about my physics project with laurel collins <3 <3

K, I say, and stuff my phone back in my poorly repaired pocket. It rests snugly against the staples, and I put my gloves back on. Physics project. Sounds more like a new conquest to me. That's good, though. It's good. Syd is always happiest when she's basking in something (someone) new.

And now I texted her first. And she's busy.

So that absolves me of my next move.

STRICKLAND'S GYM USED TO BE A DOLL SHOP. Rows and rows of dolls suffocated in boxes or breathing free on shelves. They were the creepy porcelain kind, with dead eyes and old-fashioned ruffles. Their feet dangled. The lace on their sleeves hid their hands.

You can't trust someone if you can't see their hands.

My mother used to ask if I wanted to go in, and I always refused. I wonder if she knew why. If she realized that I felt all those dead eyes on me when I got close, that the powdery smell of the air made me sick to my stomach. She must not have. Otherwise, she wouldn't have kept asking.

Anyway, I guess there's only so big a market for scary, possessed, potential murder dolls, because the place went out of business a couple of years ago, and this gym popped up inside it.

Standing outside, I hold two cups of coffee and watch Hailey through the glass.

She rubs her hands together and squares her shoulders. In one smooth stroke, she dips down and picks up a barbell, then hefts it up. Her arms don't tremble when she holds it at chest level. The muscles shift gracefully when she raises the weight over her head.

Her whole body is studied action under the effort. It's not just her arms holding the barbells aloft. It's strength in her hips and thighs that tighten above calves that curve dramatically. Her face is studied and smooth, but the muscles in her neck stand out in relief.

I'm not sure how long she holds that pose, but it's almost a shock when the barbell comes down. It bounces on the ground and Hailey rises up, all soft curves once more.

Creeper, I call myself, and open the gym door.

Humid, human heat pours over me. I smell bodies and effort and iron. Grunts and clangs compete beneath the classic rock stylings spilling out of tall speakers in the corners. Everywhere that isn't weights is glass; it's mirrors.

Confronted by myself at every angle, I feel elbowy and out of place. No one looks at me, but if they did, they'd see my scar first and then cut through my clothes down to my skin. They'd know my body isn't sculpted like an ancient Greek kouros; I'm a smooth-angled, androgynous kore at best.

Which is to say, I don't belong here; I'm the wrong shape, *and* I'm the genius who thought somebody working out might want a hot coffee.

(Stupid, stupid, stupid.)

Hailey catches sight of me in her wall o' scrutiny. She smiles, but she looks confused, too. She steps back from the barbell. Sweat makes her glow, her skin interrupted twice: black spandex boy shorts and a black spandex half shirt. She scrubs her face with a black towel, then turns toward me. "This is a surprise."

"Bad surprise?" I ask, stuck in place in my thick coat and double-cup grip.

Velcro crackles when she peels off her fingerless gloves. She crackles as she looks me over. "Not at all."

"I was in town," I say. (Truthfully, I was in town. Right after I ran through the woods. Like I said, I'm an honest liar. A piece of the truth, always a piece.) Then I say, as if it's not obvious, "I brought you a useless coffee."

That makes Hailey laugh. Her nose crinkles, gathering up faint freckles at the bridge. Her front teeth are flat, and the canines kind of stick out, and the crookedness of her smile makes it perfect. "I was just thinking that I could go for a useless coffee."

I don't offer her the cup, but I curl mine against my chest. "Yeah, I don't know what I was thinking."

"It's okay," she says. "It's sweet."

The air is too thick to breathe. Suddenly, I'm aware of the sweat caught between my clothes and my skin. My coat turns my body into a sauna, and I'm swimming in my own steam. *It's sweet* rattles in my head and shakes down my bones. Not nice or funny or any of those other friendly, distancing words. *Sweet.*

Everything is slow motion around Hailey. I watch her in the mirror as she loosens her hair and shakes it out, only to tie it up again. While she tells me about her workout, I watch the nape of her neck in the glass. I memorize the shape of her hair when it's pulled tight.

She pulls on a hoodie. Right in front of me, she steps into

sweatpants produced from her gym bag. In go her gloves, her wristbands; one pair of shoes traded for another.

Wiping down the barbells, Hailey says, “I’m heading out; do you want a ride?”

Jane stands beside me in the mirror. A black line runs through her, the space between one panel and another. She’s uneven, right side higher than the left, the buttons on her jacket out of place against the holes. She stares at me: *Make up your mind, loser.*

“That would be great,” I say.

I TEXT MY MOTHER, Out with Hailey.

She doesn't reply for a long time, and I don't sit on top of my phone waiting for it, either. It's so cold out that Hailey makes her own windows fog up. It's the heat from working out still radiating from her body. She cracks a window. The wind immediately steals a lock of her hair.

Out of nowhere, I say, "I love driving when it's getting dark. It feels like flying."

"I dream about flying," Hailey says.

"Are you in something? To do the flying, I mean. Like a plane or a car—cars don't fly, but you know what I mean."

She smiles the softest smile. It looks like a dream, like she just stepped out of sleep. "No, it's just me. Sometimes I'm standing on a cliff, and the ocean is like, 'Jump.' And I'm afraid, because of the rocks, you know? But the ocean is like, 'If you fall, I'll catch you.' So I jump. And I don't fall."

That dream, out in the world, feels so real right now. My skin prickles, the way it does when I stand close to the water when it's cold and dark and wide.

We skim a curve, the sunset glimmering through the reach of leafless trees. There's no road, no sky, nothing but speed. Nothing but Hailey's hair, flying free in the wind, and the cold on my face. With a thin breath, I say, "That . . . is the best dream ever."

"It's sad to wake up," she says. "Finding out it's not real."

Dreams crack like thin ice, but this—this moment—can go on, if we let it.

I want to stay right here, her perfume clinging to my hair. Flying into twilight, going nowhere. I want it like I want food and sleep and new books and new ink. "You want to keep driving?" I ask.

Hailey glances at me, a flash, a light. Then her eyes are back on the road, fixed and certain. "I always wondered what was at the end of this road, this one up here."

"Take it."

The turn signal glows on the snow. The tires groan; we cut the corner short, and a fir brushes the door like a car wash.

This road isn't plowed like the main one. There are probably two lanes on a good day, but right now, there's a messy rut to follow, the path cleared by other drivers during the day.

Hailey slows, putting her hand on the gearshift. I don't drive, but I've seen my mom do it a thousand times. Even an automatic has first and second gear, ideal for control when the snow is high and the roads are slick.

Trees grow up and over this road. Barely breathing and full of strange expectations, I take it in. Bare limbs cast a net between the ground and the stars. The pines fill in between, gathering dark.

It's a tunnel, one that lives and shifts and breathes. As we venture deeper into it, I feel the real world slip away.

"It looks like a holloway," I murmur.

The snow deepens; Hailey shifts into second. "What's that?"

"Old roads. The oldest roads . . . trails walked before cities. Time passed, new roads were built, you know. But that old trail is so worn, it's lower than the ground on either side. Everything grows up around it. Ancient trees that spread their branches so far overhead it looks like . . ."

"Like this." Hailey smiles.

"Yeah," I say. "Just like this."

I'm breathless as the road narrows. Our flight lands, and we creep down the middle of the road. The dark presses in, but we press back. Nothing can stop us; this is an adventure. Our journey into Hades, to see if we can return without looking back. Our march toward Russia in winter. Nobody's come back before, but is that really a good reason to stay home?

"Do you see that?" Hailey asks.

Leaning forward, I squint into the distance. For a while now, I haven't seen anything but the curve of Hailey's lower lip in the dark. It takes me a second to figure out what she means, but then I see it.

I would have mistaken it for a fall of trees, if I'd seen it at all. Spindly legs stretch above the trees on a high point, crosshatched with uneven strokes. The shape swirls into my head, assembling itself until I recognize it.

"Oh," I say, still leaning forward. "I think it's an old fire tower."

"Seriously?"

She sounds awed and excited. And without warning, she drops the Bug into first. The car shudders a little as we veer toward a nonexistent shoulder. It takes no effort to stop; we're pointing up an incline and we were going four miles an hour anyway.

Hailey crunches the parking brake into position, then opens her door. When she turns toward me, the wind sighs behind her and her hair floats loose around her face. She says, "Come on," and backs out of the car.

There's no way I can open my door. Hailey knows that; she leans back in and offers me a hand. Stripping off my seat belt, I hesitate, then reach out. Beneath a soft knit glove, Hailey's hand is sure and strong. Her fingers close around mine, and she waits to pull until I've hefted myself over the gearshift and brake. She pulls me to my feet smoothly.

Our bodies collide, not hard. Just on a thermonuclear scale, my atoms and her atoms brushing and expanding.

It's possible I step out of the way of the door; equally possible that she pulls me out of the way. Either way, she closes it, then takes off toward the fire tower. I trail her. She hasn't let go of my hand; I don't want her to.

It's full dark now. The sky still wears that almost purple edging, the sun's last signature after setting. I'm not sure where the moon is, but it must be out. It must be bright. The snow glows, and it can't do that without a light to reflect.

The fire tower is deeper in the woods and farther up the hill than it seemed at first. It's a long run through Wonderland to get to it. We feel very late to an important date.

The trees actually fall away when we reach the peak with the tower. The ground around it is thick with snow—all from last night. We stop at the edge of the clearing, shoulder to shoulder, elbow

(Things I Can)

to elbow, hands linked. Both of us tip our heads back at the same time. A narrow flight of stairs resolves into a ladder. That ladder leads into a little box, a little house on stilts in the middle of nowhere.

Hailey and I breathe hard.

"Let's climb it," I say recklessly.

Hailey looks to me. She doesn't ask, "Are you sure?" She doesn't protest, "We probably shouldn't." No, her eyes burn bright, and she smiles in wonder. Like maybe she was thinking the same thing, and I'm just the one who said the words out loud. Like maybe this is as close to flying as we'll both get outside our dreams.

Since I cast the words into the air, I squeeze her hand and go first. There's a little gate at the bottom of the stairs, but it's not locked. Just a little latch that lifts easily, and I step onto the platform from the bottom.

Clutching both rails, I take a couple steps. Then I stop and jump up and down. My heart all but explodes in my chest. This is crazy; this is dangerous. Except, it doesn't seem dangerous, and I look back at Hailey, exhilarated. "Sturdy."

"Go, go, go," she says. She plants a hand in the middle of my back.

She doesn't push, but I move anyway. The stairs are narrow,

barely wider than my hips. They cage me in, tight and safe as I ascend. I get dizzy when they double back on themselves, then back again, a wide spiral almost to the top of the tower.

When they stop, it's on a platform where the ladder rests. The wind pulls harder here. The tower sways. For the first time, I taste fear.

It's like climbing a pine tree. The branches are so close together at the bottom, so thick. They're practically steps; it feels like you could walk on up. But then you get higher; the trunk grows thinner. The wind kicks up and everything sways. You sway; the spindle snaps.

That's when you realize, you don't climb pines! They bend. They break. You hit every branch on the way down. But I refuse to think about how far down the ground is. Hailey's at my heels, and all I want to do is climb on.

At the top of the ladder, a hatch. I have to hang on to a rung with one hand and twist a bolt with the other to get it open. The hatch gives, but it's still heavy. Bowing my head, I press against it with my shoulder and use my body to lever it open. I clamber into an attic. When I get to my feet, I duck preemptively. I turn back and offer Hailey my hand this time.

She springs up, and we collide again. She laughs, rubbing her hands down my arms, then spins away. There's a roof, but the walls only go halfway up. The rest is open: to the wind, to the sky, to the stars. The tower sways beneath our feet, and I catch one of the beams, just in case.

"Oh, wow," Hailey murmurs.

I press next to her; I look out with her. Suddenly, there's nothing but a glittered sky and treetops for miles around. They ripple and wave, so dense it seems like we should be able to walk across them. So solid it feels like we made it to the other side, to another universe, to another dimension.

Trying to orient myself, I look back where I think we left the car. It's gone. Everything's gone. The world is wiped away. This tower, these two bodies, that's all that exists in this world right now.

(three three there are three bodies)

I put my hand down on top of Hailey's, on purpose. Everything cold flies away when she turns her hand beneath mine. Our fingers tangle; our heat expands. We say nothing as we look into infinity, because infinity looks back into us.

The wind blows.

WHEN I ROLL IN, MOM CALLS OUT, "AVA?"

I'm not sure who else it would be. To be fair, though, I don't feel like my usual me. I feel *light*. Not trudgey or slow. This bubbly, erratic version of myself closes the door and falls back against it. She calls back to Mom, "Sorry, ma'am, this is Joe Robber, Esquire. I'm here for your TV and MacBook."

My mother snorts from the kitchen. "You're too late, Joe Robber. In fact, you were supposed to be home half an hour ago."

"Sorry," I say, not really.

"There's potpie in the microwave."

Leftovers from a pitch-in at work, I guess. There's no way Mom made a potpie between the time she got home and the time I did. Scratch that—there's no way Mom made a potpie, full stop.

Peeling out of my coat and gloves, I let them slump on the bench by the door and go to explore.

In the kitchen, Mom stands over the island. Her dinner sits in front of her, and she picks at it as she reads something on her phone. When I pass, I see the flash of pages. Something on her library app, probably a romance novel. I'm guessing it concerns a tempestuous Scottish laird and a fiery English orphan (who turns out to be nobility).

Mom loves history, too, just in her own way.

"Did you have fun with . . . Hailey?" she asks. She abandons her phone, watching me and blindly pulling a plate from the cabinet.

"Yes."

Mom frowns. It's not dismay; she just expected more. Details, an explanation, embroidery. She's probably trying to place Hailey—where does she exist in my past, in my circle? Swinging open the microwave door, Mom finally asks, "Is that Matthew Cho's daughter?"

A power surge pops inside me. I haven't made her up. She exists when I'm not thinking about her; she has a history, a past, a life, a family. For one halogen moment, I'm reminded why my mom knows Matthew Cho, but I drown that thought with my own, new light. I'm too bright, too brand-new with a sudden surge of energy; I blot out everything. I say, "Yeah. She's doing strength training downtown, and I went to watch."

(After I went down to the riverside.

After I chased the boy.

Before the drive, before flying, before the other world.)

"Strength training?" What Mom doesn't say is, *Since when do you care about strength training? And why would you want to watch it?*

With a wave of my hand, I dismiss her furrowed brow. "Yeah, it's for endurance. She's really good at it." (I assume. I mean, she didn't drop anything.)

(Well, she did. But it was on purpose.)

"Huh," she says. "I didn't know you two were close."

Oh, we were close, Mom. We were *so* close on the top of the fire tower. We were one huddled shape, hands laced together, trying to figure out which way was Canada and which way was the car. We were so close that my lips ached, because her lips were parted and gleaming with Carmex. Camphor and cedar and new storm wind; I drank in her traces in the towering dark.

I shrug. "We eat lunch together."

My mom nods and returns to her book. "Next time, text me if you're going to be this late. I don't really like you coming in after dark."

Next time.

Not only does Hailey exist in the bigger world, at home with parents, she exists *in the future*. In *my* future. I'm so dizzy, it takes two tries to get my plate into the microwave. I play the buttons like a harpsichord, then take a turn on my heel. Frictionless, I spin.

Just once. Before my mother can look up from her iPhone and catch me.

I can't (don't want to) explain that much exuberance. It's mine. It's all mine, a secret tattooed nowhere but my heart.

MY BODY HAS A COMPLICATED STING.

As always, I turn the shower up too hot, so hot that I huddle at one end of the tub and risk scalding as I turn it down to bearable.

When I duck under the spray, I gasp. It's still shockingly hot but in a good way. I like the bite of heat on the back of my neck. The way water gathers in my hair, then pulls it to a point. Rivers spill down my spine and split across my breasts.

I have washcloths, right there in the little closet inside the bathroom. Pale peach, matching the bath sheets and hand towels. But I never wash with a rag, never. The rasp feels clinical, chemical—I hate it; I don't use one. Even the word, I hate the word. "Rag," so hard and brassy and braying.

Instead, I lather the soap in my hands to wash my face and neck. Skin on skin, quick swirls, a splash of scalding water. Then the rest of me, I scrub with the bar itself.

Turning my back to the water, I wash with curved fingers and disappear into my head. My thoughts are a slide show.

Abstract: the ripple of Hailey's knuckles inside her black, fingerless gloves. The window, rolled down enough to give up her hair to the elements. Her smile, perfectly crooked with her little vampire teeth exposed.

She's funny and strange; she wants to fly. She drives with strangers in the dark.

My hands drift on soap currents, shaping the weight of my breasts, straying between my soft thighs. The little ache there throbs, but I pass by. Instead, I turn beneath the water and let molten fire spill across my sensitive skin.

Because I have to, I wash my hair quickly, then cut the water. Soaking wet, I scrub my head with a towel. I give my skin a cursory swipe, then wrap peach terry cloth around my body. When I walk across the hallway to my bedroom, I'm quick. I leave only footprints behind, and I lock my bedroom door.

The right water is hard to find. I gave up a while ago. I don't like my fingers because I concentrate too hard and rub too hard and get nowhere. But the magic of an allowance, the existence of Visa gift cards, and the open road of the internet mean I don't have to use my hands.

Turning out my light, I slide into bed, still wrapped in the towel.

Then I dig between the mattress and box spring until I find my familiar friend. Mine is boring compared to some of the crazy things that come up on Amazon when you type *vibrator* into the search engine. There are no beads or pearls or colors or natural replications here; it's just a slim white tube with a twist base on it.

It's quiet, like prayer; even quieter beneath my covers and towel. Only on the outside, the shaft pressed against flesh and bone, its tip infiltrates dark curls and parts lips to find my clitoris. When I find the spot, my feet twist and curve. One heel digs into the mattress like an anchor.

My body is strange and ordinary; it races with sensation but waits for my brain. And my brain is just plain strange. I don't do this and think about people. I never have. Instead, I try to convince my mind to wander. To find images and shapes and impressions, pleasant but unformed. My thoughts turn to water, swirling in currents and coming in waves. Sometimes—not tonight—but sometimes, I read. Fanfic and history books and dystopian novels; not usually, almost never, stuff about sex. It's just *stuff.* It makes my mind forget what my body is doing so my body can do its wonderful thing.

Because there's danger in there. I can't concentrate on the thing or I frustrate myself. It doesn't happen; it's all kindling, no fire. It grinds my teeth, and do you know how hard it is to fall asleep when you're mad at your own flesh?

So I can't concentrate, but I can't let my mind go lazy, go blank. Alone, in the dark, yearning and wanting, my brain decides it needs to think about something. It plucks out memories I don't want to have.

(something that feels good in the summer)

My brain kicks open the box just to watch the bloodbath.

People freaking joke about good-touch/bad-touch, and it's not funny. Good-touch dissolves into old hands-dirty hands-bad hands everywhere; rancid air I've already breathed; hot, swollen summer moments I never want back.

When the bloodbath happens, my spine coils like steel line. My jaw sets hard; my heel digs in harder. I open my eyes wide, staring at my ceiling as if I could burn through it with a gaze. And I talk. Low and furious—out loud.

"Stop it."

"Shut up."

"Not that."

And I banish it. I banish him. Because this is my body, and he's not invited. My heart beats thready and uneven. It takes a little while (a long time) to get my mind clean and unfocused again.

Sometimes here I give up. Too much trouble. Too hard to let go . . .

Sometimes ~~it~~ **he** won't go away, and I stop, and I hold so very still under my sheets. I try not to breathe hard. I hide from my past by making myself small in my own bed.

If my thoughts *do* blur again, I concentrate but don't concentrate. Yes, that color; yes, that sudden thread of a thought that feels like a kiss. Yes, that phantom hand that belongs to no one, but someone safe and good—that imaginary touch can go on. I urge it; I encourage it.

If things veer dark, I force them back to light. Close. So close, and everything goes broad and dark as the universe around me. Everything in me collapses, a dying star that becomes a pinpoint before exploding in one spectacular corona. My steel spine arches; my teeth cut my lips. I touch the live wire, and then I let go.

Afterward, sometimes, I'm relaxed enough to just *be.* My thoughts flow in safe, lazy rivers, and I think about everything, anything. Sometimes history. Sometimes shower thoughts, like *Isn't it crazy that the brain named itself?*

But tonight, on this particular night, I think about how I got here, breathing fast and body jellied beneath my sheets. I flew, down a dark road; I flew with *her*. For a moment, I'm cured. And then, in a moment, I'm no longer alone.

Jane lies beside me; the ghost of her weight fills the pillow beside me. I roll onto my side and curl up, tight, tight, tight. I hold pleasure and happiness and joy inside. I knot them in with my body. Tense again but like a hug.

"See," Jane murmurs in the dark, glowing like the winter moon. "You're fine."

"I'm fine," I agree.

Her lips barely moving, she says, "I am *not*."

I nod, still holding myself tight. "But I'll take care of you."

Suddenly, Jane smiles.

"IT'S COLD," SHE SAYS.

I scrub a hand over my face, sitting up in my empty bed. I didn't dream the voice; it didn't wake me up, either. A burn in my throat, the frozen stiffness of my breath in my nose—that's what woke me. Colonies of ice spread beneath my skin, and I swear I can see my breath in the air.

Jane's call pierces, plunging into my flesh. It puts hooks into me. It pricks and bites, dragging me up to stare into the darkness. There's an urgency in my head, in my hands. I throw off my covers, but I still have to untangle the towel around me. The humidity inside it escapes, and I shiver.

Jane's calling. From the dark. From the cold. And I feel that thin sliver bisecting my heart. Her grave seems lonely, but it's not. Someone else was there. She said she wasn't fine, and she's not. Someone put her there.

What if they're back? What if they take her? What if they touch her? What if, what if, what if—?

Stop. Focus. Sweatshirt, I need a sweatshirt. In the bottom drawer; sweatpants, too. Maybe I should pull on my only pair of long johns first? Yes. Do that.

(this is not absurd. i am not crazy.)

(i promised to take care of her.)

Socks—*boot* socks. Nice and thick, scratching at the place where I missed shaving on my ankle.

I don't think; it's a gift, this connection. I don't consider the voice. Right now, I just dress—because I need to dress. Done.

Downstairs. I drag on my coat, and I reach into the pockets. No gloves. Are they in Hailey's car? I know I had them on at the fire tower because our skin was so close and so far away. Why would I take them off in the car? A forget-me-not? An excuse for another ride?

I'm disappointed in myself when I find my gloves sitting on the floor under the coat hooks. I'm not secretly clever, it turns out. Just clumsy/messy/careless. Gloves on, and then I cram a hat on my head. Beneath the knit, I feel the trace of moisture—my hair, not quite dry.

The spare keys to my mom's car hang by the door. On a hook shaped like a crooked finger, actually. My dad's idea of a joke, but it always scared me.

The dark, almost rusted metal seems to thrust out from the wall. I always expected it to start moving, tearing, unwrapping the walls of my house, to make a space big enough to escape. Fingers belong to hands. Hands belong to bodies, and bodies—

(She's cold.)

Here's the thing. I don't drive. I don't mean I *can't.* I took Driver's Ed and then an extra Driver's Ed outside of school and went out with my parents on errands.

Dad tried to hide his annoyance when I didn't do exactly what I was supposed to at the moment he thought I should do it. Mom, on the other hand, gasped. Brake too hard, *gasp*. Turn too fast, *gasp*. Try to parallel park, *gasp gasp gasp*.

"Sorry," she'd say. "You're doing fine."

Gasp.

So I just . . . never got my license. Mom didn't push the issue, and Dad had moved to Mount Desert by then.

But I *can* drive.

Holding the door to the garage open a few inches, I press myself through it like I'm sausage. So slowly, I lean against the door to close it. Silent; I need it to latch in silence.

When it's closed, I creep along the length of Mom's car to the actual garage door. If I push the button, the opener will grind to life, and that thing plays like an orchestra of the damned.

I rise on my toes to release the hook at the top. Then I carefully, slowly, *slowly* push the door open. It rolls smoothly, rattling just enough to make me nervous. Once it's up and open, I still. Snow sweeps into the garage as I listen to my house. Listen for my mother. Winter is a scourge, the wind like biting chains. All I hear is the night, the wind, the creep and groan of settling snow.

Into the car, key in slot, lights turned off. People in movies know how to pop the engine, just enough to throw it in neutral and roll from a garage in silence. For a second, I think I could try that.

No, I can't. I just put it in reverse and back out carefully. I try to stay in the tracks Mom left on the driveway. They're already half full, and I panic when I lose traction for a second. The tires spin; the engine whines.

Oh god, getting stuck in the snow, murdering the escape before it begins; that's just not an option. I'm going to be in a legendary amount of trouble if I get caught. At the very least, I should get in trouble for what I do, not what I tried to do.

Finally on the road, I turn on the headlights. From the corner of my eye, I see the dark maw of my garage, standing open. I'm just going to leave it. Leave the house vulnerable. Leave the door basically open, for anyone to just walk in while I'm gone. I'm—

Going to run back up to the garage and pull the door down. It comes down hard, with a crash that cracks like thunder down the street. Now the adrenaline kicks in. I run back to the car and take off.

The seat belt locks on me when I skid to a stop at the first sign. It's an iron band, fixing me in the seat. The bar's down on this roller coaster now. I have no choice: I just have to ride.

The streets are deserted. Salt trucks and plows are probably running somewhere—the road I'm on has a ghost layer of snow. No one drives past; no one tailgates me even though I'm doing at least ten miles under the limit. I have to do this, but I can't believe I'm doing this. Tight shoulders translate to tight hands on the wheel.

My breath hazes the air. I'm afraid to take my hands off ten and two, but the windshield is starting to fog over. When I turn onto the big road, my stomach tightens. There *are* people here, mostly zooming past in the other direction.

The trucks make Mom's little car rock in their wake. At this angle, the wind pushes, too. I feel it in the wheel; I have to fight against it to stay straight and true.

The thing I was hiding from myself starts to show. Down here, down one of these curves, is the place.

The headlights reflect off the snow but disappear into the asphalt. This doesn't feel like flying at all. It's tunneling, digging through the dark, hoping to sense the destination.

All the stitches that hold me together from the inside fray. They dangle and trail; they twist together, tangling and knotting. They wrap a garrote around my heart and tighten it-tighten it-tighten it. I breathe, but I'm not getting air.

Driving without a license. Going to see a dead girl in the middle of the night. What is wrong with me? What the— the headlights illuminate a body

(a person)

standing on the side of the road. Thumb out, hunched into her jean jacket.

Jane.

Out of her grave. Dressed. She's not dressed for the weather, though. Her hands are bare; so's her head. The wind pulls her hair in a storm around her face. When she looks up, her eyes aren't blue or green or brown or hazel. They're blotted out with a black stripe across the whites.

Shocked, I slam on the brakes. No control at all anymore; the car fishtails. The tires whine; the belt bites my shoulder. *Oh god oh god oh god I'm going to hit her, a tree, a boulder, the guardrail, oh god!* My head whips forward, then back. The car shudders to a stop.

Twice I fumble before I get the car into park. Three times before I get the doors open, and I lower the window because I can't remember if the car locks automatically when somebody gets out. I can't remember any of these things because I *don't drive.* I don't go out by myself. I don't go out at night. I don't do any of these things, ever, *ever.*

The seat belt releases with a pop, and I fall out of the car. My legs don't believe in weight right now. *God, was that her? Was that someone else?! Did I hit her? Did I kill her?* My keys shake out of my hands. I step on them to get to the front of the car. *What did I do? What have I done?! Do it. Look. Look, Ava.*

I do. I look over the hood. I look to where Jane isn't. She's gone.

And now I don't know if she was ever there.

WITH MY MOM'S EMERGENCY FLASHLIGHT IN HAND, I descend into the trees.

I keep my phone on in my other hand, following my map to get to her. Jane rests somewhere between two staggered, walking loops. She's the X that marks the spot. The perverse treasure at the end of a midnight rainbow. She was in my bed and a vision in the road, and now I have to check on her. I promised. I swore.

After the skid-out on the road, I'm more careful. I choose each step so I fall less; a brave sort of stupidity overtakes me. Hannibal couldn't do it; Napoleon couldn't do it; Hitler couldn't do it. But I'm going to invade Russia in the winter, and I'm going to succeed. The trick is lowered expectations and a pathological level of self-delusion.

(Probably the other guys had that, too.)

I've been in these woods so much lately, they almost feel welcoming. Winter is quiet. Not many birds call and answer. Few rabbits, possibly only the sad domesticated ones who got dumped after Easter was over and haven't figured out that they stand out against the snow.

And listen, okay, I know this is a bad idea. I know this is

(crazy)

potentially dangerous, but

I also equally know that Jane woke me up. She might not be alone. There are two of us living who know where she is, and one of us might hurt her again. Who might feel like she belongs to him. And she doesn't. She does. Not.

She belongs to herself. Only herself. Somebody ignored that, somebody used her up, split her skin with something sharp (*a knife, was it a knife?*), and tossed her away. He doesn't get to have another piece.

He doesn't get to keep anything but memories

(and I would cut those out of his brain with a paring knife if I could; he makes my hands tremble with terrible, bloody potential).

No one else gets to hurt her. No one else—

Someone else *is* here. Again! I stop. I snap my teeth closed. I squint and sharpen my ears. There are little ticks and shifts in the snow. When I focus, I hear the river. Both the water that rushes and the ice that crackles at the banks.

Footsteps.

There are footsteps. Heavy. Human. Even when deer glide through the dark, they're light on their feet. Owls are a glimmer and a whisper, no louder than the beat of a moth's wings in flight. People stomp and tromp and curse when they get tangled in the snow-covered thicket.

I turn. I see a spark in the night. Small, probably a cell phone flashlight. The cold encases me like a shell, but inside, I flow like magma. I am fire and heat. I'm a flaming sword. It must be him.

It has to be, because who else would it be? Here, in these woods, in this spot, in the hour when Jane called to me and told me she was cold? And why? Why? Because she's exposed. Because *he's* back, exposing her.

My mouth goes sour, and my bones harden. I take a moment to watch. To plot. There must be some way to sneak up on him, to take him down. I didn't bring a weapon, but I brought my mind. I have a flashlight, heavy with a lithium battery. And I have a brain that whispers, *Run*, at the same time it urges, *Get him*.

I battle myself, and it seems almost possible that I will stand there until dawn, undecided. Until I hear a thing. Until I hear *the* thing.

The shutter snap on a cell phone.

Small lightning flashes with it.

He's taking her picture! The monster.

I roar and run toward him. Startled, he cries out. When he scrambles this time, he falls.

This time, I gain on him. This time, I'm everything I wasn't before. Swift. Sure. The frozen lash of brush against my face spurs me forward while he struggles.

As I reach him, he staggers to his feet. Tall. Taller than me. I grab for him and catch his hood. It falls; it jerks him back like a choke chain.

Pale hair, silky curls. Dark brows, a flash of dusky lips, and pale skin. I see him but don't see him. The moon remembers; the snow. He's made of snow and shadows.

He twists in my snare. Writhing and snarling, he jerks against my grasp. My shoulder burns from the force.

No. He doesn't get away. Not this time.

I swing the flashlight with my free hand. It just bounces off his coat-padded shoulder. It shifts me off balance.

With a fierce tug, he yanks free. Again, he falls. Into the brambles. He howls; it hurts.

(good)

I grab for the hood again. Just out of my reach. My gloved fingers skate the canvas of his coat. When they skitter off, I catch the hem. Trying to twist it in my fist, I fail. It's too narrow. Too slick.

Lurching away from me, he stutters out, "B-b-back off!"

"I'm calling the police," I bray.

When I reach for him again, he slaps my hands away. Even as he drags up the ravine, he swings an arm behind him. It's wild, unfocused. Like the head of a mace, just spinning and spinning, hoping to hit something.

Instead, I catch his wrist.

The force jerks him off his feet; me too. He sprawls on his back, and I go down. Gravity drags him toward the river. For a second, the sky is the ground, and the ground is just formless, falling space. His cell phone bursts into light when it hits the snow.

Suddenly, fear exists again. I don't want to fall. I don't want to end up in the icy Aroostook in the dark. I let go. I slide to a stop, and I'm aware.

The ground beneath me exists again, too. It's hard. I'm cold. My head rests against a rock. My stupid, brave, fearless brain whispers, *You could have died; you almost died.*

And in that moment of my hesitation, the boy regains his feet and runs.

Flailing to sit up, I scream after him, "I know what you did! I see her, and I know what you did!"

And then blinking light.

From his cell phone,

where it sits just in front of me

in the snow.

NOW MAYBE YOU'RE WONDERING, *IS AVA HAVING A breakdown?*

No, I tell you, referring to myself in the third person, Ava is not having a breakdown. Maybe a break*through.*

Jane woke me up. She called me to her because she knew I'd catch him there. Since we have this terrible thing in common, we are bound together, she and I. There is a power that flows between us, and I have to use it for good. For once, for good.

Disappointment tinges everything I taste. Just a bitter dust, imperceptible to the eye. If I'd been stronger, maybe I would have caught him.

In retrospect, though, so what if I had? Even if I had held on to him, what would have happened then? He was taller, bigger—we fell to the river's edge.

I had no plan.

Clock him with the flashlight again? Hope he goes down like they do in the movies? Hope I had the strength to drag him all the way into town? Or hope he didn't wake up before the police *whom I didn't want to call* showed up?

It doesn't matter. I will catch him.

I just wasn't supposed to catch him yet.

The cold clings to my skin, even after a second shower. My alarm will ring soon. Time for school. Time to greet the day. His phone lies heavy in my hand. I sit on the side of my bed and stare down at it. Well, actually, I'm staring at a grid of dots.

His password is a shape. And just beyond that digital portcullis, there's everything. I know he has pictures of her from tonight. There are probably more. Somebody like that, who goes back to the grave for another memento, he has others. It wasn't enough to

(destroy)

hurt her and hide her and keep his sick memories of her. She is dead and he wants to keep using her. He keeps using her, and this phone is *evidence.*

I could take it to the police, now. There's enough to hand it over, take my hands off the wheel, and let it just go.

But it's time for school.

I need makeup today. That slide down the ravine left a bruise on my cheek that I don't want to explain. Hopefully, it won't get darker.

"YEAH," I SAY TO SYD, LEANING OVER HER IN THE cafeteria. "I found it, and I figured you might be able to crack it."

The phone lies on the table in front of her, and she studies it like she's defusing a bomb. Probably I shouldn't even *think* bomb in school. I don't need to get arrested over a bad choice of words.

Around us, people move in their conversations and don't even notice us. I'm not sure why I expect something different. We're just two people looking at a phone. There are mirrors of us everywhere, spread out with Starbucks cups and the remains of stale school donuts.

Still, I expect (*fear? anticipate?*) notice, so I sit down with Syd, pressing close to her. "What do you think?"

Syd holds it level to her gaze, tipping it slightly to one side, then the other. "It's pretty messed up."

"I know," I say. "I found it outside."

I don't know why I feel like I have to justify that. I found a lost phone. I found a thing. It's just a thing I found. The longer she holds it, the edgier I get. The thing is, Syd is a genius at stuff like this. Forget your password, lose your log-in, whatever. She can figure it out.

But I don't know what she might see this time if she gets past the lockscreen. I don't want to pull her in. And it feels wrong to ask her for a favor when, one, I'm not going to tell her the truth about why I need it and two, when we're so weird right now.

"I'm just going to take it to Lost and Found," I say, reaching for it.

She fends me off with her shoulder. "Ah-ah, I'm working here."

My hands twitch. I sew my mouth closed. I don't want her to be suspicious. Just like I don't want all these people, milling in the breakfast remains of the cafeteria, looking my way. Why are they all looking my way? I wish I'd left my coat in my locker. It's so hot in here. I'm sweating beneath my sweater.

"Ava, hey," Hailey says, right behind me.

Syd and I both turn to look at her. My smile is uneasy but real. The beginning of last night rises up, prickling on my skin. Hailey's hand on mine, flying in the dark, looking at a new kingdom together. Syd doesn't know about that. And Syd's expression doesn't change.

"Hey," I say. I'm not sure if I drew it out. Did I sound pervy? Does she know what's fluttering inside me, not just in my heart but down in my belly? Can she tell that I went places with her in my mind? "What's up?"

Resting her hip against the table, she returns my smile. "I was going to ask you that."

My gaze flicks to the phone. "Oh, uh . . ."

"She found it." Syd provides my voice but not my inflection. She's flat and informative, and more than a little dismissive. "We're trying to figure out whose it is."

"Oooh, maybe I can help."

Hailey slides onto the bench beside me. Sandwiched between them, I'm unbearably hot. I really should have left my coat in the locker (and kept the phone to myself).

"Can I see?" Hailey asks. She holds out her hand in front of me. It's so close, I smell her perfume. It's warm on her pulse. It seems to waft into the air with every heartbeat. It's a silver-dark cloud that swirls around my head.

Syd drops the phone into Hailey's palm. "Knock yourself out."

"Did you do the trig extra credit?" Hailey's talking to Syd, because I'm taking calc. "I couldn't figure out number three."

"Yeah, me either." Still flat, Syd's voice carries an edge. The lack of emotion bristles through her consonants and crushes her vowels.

I think Hailey notices. No. That's stupid. Hailey *obviously* notices. It's like a neon sign flashing over Syd's head. But Hailey keeps her smile on; she stays light—she floats on her cloud. She produces a bag from her backpack and unzips it. The scent of her perfume grows stronger as she rummages in it, and I sit in a tense and intoxicated place.

There's no reason for Syd to hate Hailey. At least, no reason I know. And until recently, I would have felt confident thinking that. Thinking I knew everything about Syd and what's in her head and her heart.

Maybe later, I'll ask her. Maybe later, I'll ask for a ride home and pay for pizza and make her spill her guts.

Hailey twists the lid off a pot of loose powder. Dipping a fat scarlet brush into it, she says, "Learned this from my dad. Let's see if it works."

With a tap, she leaves some of the powder in the pot and then turns to the phone. Dusting it gently, she twirls and twists, her touch so delicate that I'm not even sure the brush touches the screen. But slowly, surely, a faint translucent haze covers the glass. And when she puts the brush aside, we lean in.

There's a pattern in the powder. Faint but there. Right over the portcullis: a G-shaped ghost that beckons.

Exhaling softly, I say, "You're a genius."

Abruptly, Syd stands. Her bag swings and thumps against my back. Her earrings jingle and her nails tick on the table as she steps out of the bench. She feels like stone: a statue set to motion. Everything about her is angular, including the cut of her eyes. "I forgot. I gotta talk to Mr. Burkhart before class."

Syd walks away, right in the middle of me saying, "Okay, see you later."

"Wow."

Offended, Hailey watches Syd's retreat. A thin shell of ice crackles around her, impossible to ignore.

"I don't know what that's about," I say. I turn back to Hailey, apologetic for something I didn't even do. "She's been in her own head lately."

With a shrug, Hailey forces a smile. "It's okay." She packs away her powder, with a lying smile. "I butted in. Anyway, I have

English in the dungeon, so I should probably head that way."

I don't know what to do. I don't know the right words to make her stay, and I can't fix what Syd did.

Fumbling around, I manage to stand up the same time Hailey does. It feels like desperation and I'm afraid it sounds like it, too, but I say, "I'll walk with you!"

The lie slips from her smile.

AS WE WALK DOWN THE HALL, OUR FINGERS FLICKER and tease.

They don't link; instead, they stroke. We talk about the weather, the forecast—more snow, so much snow, a million tons of snow—as if our hands aren't stretching and reaching for something more between us.

A little realization springs up between those touches. Her knuckles skim mine, deliberate. My forefinger

(no bigger than the agate stone on the forefinger of an alderman)

curls and kisses the pad of hers. Our elaborate dance is subtle. It has no feathers. It has no display. It's murmurings under covers and whispers in shadows.

It's for us, alone, because maybe Hailey *knows*, but I'm *discovering*. I've had crushes on people before—oblique longings over impossible boys and girls, over smooth stars androgynously male and female. But.

But no one I could touch. No one who could touch me.

(Are you thinking, *Ohhh, because . . . ?* Because no. And yes. Everything can't be about that, but everything is touched by that.

But also, other things—*other* other things. Syd got her period in fifth grade; I didn't get mine until freshman year. Her first crush-kiss-ginity flew away in middle school; as I recall, at Tenesta Jordan's thirteenth birthday party.

I didn't go to parties or sleepovers or anywhere to meet people but school (and a lot of people at school know, or think they know, what happened because we were going to school together when it happened, and it sets me apart and makes me damaged in *their* minds, their tiny little minds), and besides which, at school there are *too many people* around all the time. Too much close, too much loud.

And maybe I could find a group of new kids who didn't know all that, but don't forget, I have a huge scar running down the side of my face. When new people see me for the first time, they're shocked/disgusted/revolted, which makes me feel so, so, *so* very pretty and inclined to flirt, you know?

Never mind the conversation that follows: *What happened to you—?*

It's all a big circle, isn't it? A snake swallowing its tail. A Möbius strip of why Ava is seventeen and currently losing her *mind* over four fingers curled against four fingers, in the dank hallway of the school's basement.)

Bravery and madness and because it's my right arm, which falls under *Things I Can*, I turn my hand, and slip it into Hailey's. Contact. Heat. When her fingers close around mine, sensation sizzles all the way to my toes. It burns like a sparkler, bright hot and inevitable.

Her palm is soft; her fingertips rough. I wonder about her elbows, about her knees. I wonder about her surprises and the weight of her lips.

There's plenty of room around us, but she presses close to me. Squeezing my hand, she steals a look in my direction, and I blush. I warm with a smile, and I don't let go. I might imagine a gold glow around her, summer lights on her skin, but I don't think so. I believe she is *actually* luminous, there at my side.

"Do you want to go flying tonight?" I murmur.

Her hand tightens around mine again. We are close and small, hidden away from everything together. For a moment, we *are* everything. A dark seed. All matter in the universe. The moment before the big bang.

She says, "I can't tonight. Tomorrow?" and kick-starts the creation of all things.

Bang.

PREVIOUSLY MENTIONED: I DON'T CUT CLASS.

Not previously mentioned: Jane's making it impossible for me to concentrate. Everything in the lab is glittery, glassy bright, and I see her everywhere. Curve of a beaker, width of an Erlenmeyer flask, stretch of a test tube. It's like a house of mirrors, but the only reflection I see isn't mine.

Trying to ignore her, I turn my school iPad landscape-wise, and type my notes faster. The problem is, there's glass between me and canvas, so I see her there, too. She lifts her chin and waits. Raises an eyebrow and waits. Huffs a sigh that lifts her shoulders and *waits.*

So I raise my hand and ask to go to the nurse. I never ask to leave, so Mr. Fancher doesn't quiz me. I won't have to claim, out loud, that I have cramps or lie that I have a migraine or pretend to try to barf. I gather my things and slip out of chem silently.

I'm not sure where to go. Like a marble fired into a pinball machine, I move erratically through the empty hallways. Into the bathroom? No. Mirrors in there, and I already feel Jane staring at me from behind (even though there's nothing there when I turn around). No library pass, so the media center is out.

Briefly, I'm ashamed of myself. That I got to eleventh grade and I have no idea how to cut a class successfully. I'm more ashamed when I walk into the clinic and wait at the nurse's desk while she talks on the phone.

"I was in chem, and I started feeling sick," I say when she hangs up.

The nurse takes down my name, the class I vacated, and checks my temperature. It's normal, of course, but I think the combination of chemistry and sick are more powerful than 97.8 degrees on the little ear poky. She allots me a cot in the back of the clinic, where the overhead light is turned off.

It's not dark back there, just dim. She even pulls the curtain, after encouraging me to lay down and rest awhile.

Hospitals have a smell, acrid and antiseptic. But the school clinic just smells like the school, with a hint of clean laundry thrown in (the cot sheets, I'm guessing). Lying down, I actually close my eyes and try to rest for a minute. It feels less dishonest if I do as I'm told. Plus, I bet she checks on me soon. Probably to catch me on a cell phone or otherwise enjoying my time away from class.

So it's not until I hear her talking to Jacob Cassy about his insulin pump that I pull the phone from my backpack. Gingerly, I hold it by its edges. The powder is smeared; an electric quaver ripples through my chest. Fear, anxiety, but they're not necessary. Right on the screen, the pseudo Greek key design remains visible in Mineral Basics Translucent Medium.

"Do it," Jane says.

There she is, crammed onto the cot with me. In a cleft just the size of a fallen log, pressed, compressed. She makes a noise like, *Well?* So I look around; I listen.

There's the sound of an open phone line on speaker. Then numbers beeping, then ringing. When someone picks up, the speaker cuts off. The nurse asks for Mr. Cassy—

"Hurry up," Jane says.

She has reason to be impatient. He could be coming back to her anytime. He could be back there now. She urges with a cold breath against my ear. "Do it."

I sweep my finger over the pattern, and the phone squawks. It sounds like a loudspeaker, a fire alarm, an Amber Alert. Obviously, I started the pattern from the wrong end, but I really can't get caught at this. The nurse will take the phone; I'll be sent back to class.

(Will my parents be notified? I don't know! I've never been this far down the screwing-off-at-school well before.)

The volume doesn't want to turn down without being unlocked. Cradling it against my chest to muffle the sound, I start the shape over. The screen goes completely dark.

Fear flashes over me, inverse blue, like the afterimage of lighting. All the things that could be going wrong careen through my head: *security-shutdown-findmyphone.*

Instead, the screen clears. Apps appear. The wallpaper coalesces: it's not Jane's body. Thank god, thank Ishtar, thank whoever. It's just vectored swirls of color that drift into space. It's ordinary, so ordinary. The same apps anyone has, that I have, dot the screen at random. Killers use Discord chat, too.

My stomach gurgles. An acid lash spins in it as I waver between Gallery and Mail. Gallery or Mail, Mail or Gallery . . .

If he has a murder scrapbook, I don't want to look at school. I shouldn't look at it at school—

The gallery opens with a quiet *swoosh*. Three albums take a few seconds to load. It feels like forever—a long brittle strand of terrible possibility. And then, the images.

First, I find last night's album. A snowy wood. A couple of rocks that jut up at odd angles. Then, Jane's grave, still closed, still snow covered, from every angle. It looks like I ruined his plans to get more intimate with her.

Good.

The album from the night before last is blurry taillights and unfamiliar vehicles. A big muscly car in a dark green or black bears a Maine license plate out of focus. It might be inside a garage; it's hard to tell. Next, a police car in a freshly shoveled driveway, inches of snow gathered on the hood.

Finally, an album of screenshots from Discord. Pieces of conversations: 1LostMarble and ArcanePriestess talk about her crashing with him. ArcanePriestess is excited to get there. She's gonna meet OhWeeOh tonight and be there tomorrow. And then, one screen with 1LostMarble asking her, *Are you there?*

Are you there?

AP, are you okay?

Another screencap, from a conversation with OhWeeOh. 1LostMarble asks: *Did AP make it there? I haven't heard from her.*

Me either, replies OhWeeOh.

I'm worried, 1LostMarble says. *She was supposed to be there, right?*

OhWeeOh never responds.

Glancing back at Jane, I ask her with a murmur, "Arcane-Priestess?"

She smiles from the glass in the AED cabinet, her expression curious and unreadable.

There's nothing else in the gallery; nothing on the SD card, either. My fingers skate across the screen. What's weird is that there are screencaps for the Discord chat in the gallery, but the app itself is wiped clean. No log-in, no channels, nothing. With a frown, I choose Mail.

The inbox is empty.

Sent: empty.

Drafts: empty.

Trash, Archive, Folders: empty.

So I touch Compose, and I send myself a test mail. My phone vibrates almost instantly in my pocket. I open it; return address is 1LostMarble@gmail.com. No school address. No real name.

The SMS app is buried in the background, and except for a couple of notifications from the cell carrier, that's empty, too. No bookmarks in the browser, no groups in WhatsApp; it's just weird.

It's the creepiest phone I've ever looked at. It has signs of life but no soul.

Swiping from screen to screen, I find Minecraft—murderers play sandbox games—and Waze (how to get a mutilated corpse from point A to point B without getting stuck in traffic). On the last page, there's an unfamiliar icon. It looks like a microphone—maybe something for taking notes?

When I touch it, the top half of the screen is blank. The bottom has a keyboard. Sitting up, I lean over the phone and carefully touch a few letters. *Hi there.*

"HI THERE," the phone says loudly.

It's *almost* a natural voice, and it scares the crap out of me. I shove the whole thing under the thin cot pillow and collapse on top of it. Just in case, I throw my arm over my eyes, because that looks more like resting than coffin-armed stiffness. My breath rattles in the sudden silence.

There are so many nightmare reasons to have a digital voice. It could murmur, "You wanna see something that feels good in the summer?" My stomach coils; my body remembers. His hands reach up from beneath the pillow to grasp my arms. Behind me, Jane sighs at me—look what I went and did.

I bolt upright. Catch my breath.

Whatever. I text everything to myself. Pictures, chats, screenshots of all the screens. I don't know what I'm going to use them for. I just know I want them. And I know that I keep coming back to that digital voice. I feel dirty and watched, and it lingers the longer I play with the settings.

This phone is a poison pill; I shove it in my bag. I repack my boxes. Tape them up tight. Turn out the light.

When the nurse peeks in to ask how I'm feeling, I say, "Off."

That is the absolute truth.

Everything's frozen and nothing hurts. It's not even the kind of cold that burns; instead, it's a cold like silence.

All the things that live in her sink into hibernation—the bacteria, the bodies-in-bodies, royal ascents stunted because the queen is dead but the ice is thick.

She is snow white with a black mask. She is sleeping beauty without a kiss.

Summer blowflies don't fly in the winter. They don't seek spaces for eggs and future generations, and the beetles turn away, too. Their hard-shelled eggs wait for warmth, for moisture, to spring open and send forth raspy, rattling carapaces full of hunger.

(They'd love those gouges left by the knife. Doors thrown wide open to insects who crash and bash their way into flesh recently closed tight to unwelcome visitors.)

Early winter is her gift. It covers her, again and again. Dropping temperatures reset her clock. Crystals form in the tips of her fingers and the tops of her toes.

Raccoons have fingers and toes, too. They have sharp noses and sharp curiosity. They have tenacity. It's not hard to peel the wooden shell off the delectable treat that lies inside.

No, it's not hard for masked Procyon Lotor; they can crack crayfish and crabs, mollusks and eggs.

Peeling away a bit of rotting wood to get to the luscious ladyfingers inside is nothing.

Nothing.

BASICALLY, I ATTACKED SYD AS SOON AS SCHOOL WAS over.

And by attack, I mean I aggressively walked up next to her and said, "We're getting pizza." And then, also aggressively, I walked beside her toward the parking lot until she relented.

"Zoey's or Chi-Town?"

Shooting her a patented look, I make her answer that question herself. Zoey's is the only decent pizza in town. It's New York style, with the bubbly crust and giant slices that beg to be folded in half. Chi-Town is this weird deep dish-slash-thick crust that tastes like old olive oil and questionable refrigeration.

Once we're in Syd's car (actually, still the stepdad's Jeep), I buckle in and then brush her hand away from the radio. We don't need a soundtrack for this conversation. In fact, music would just make it easier to drift away from the hard stuff—suddenly I'd sing a line, and then she'd say, "I love the way he finds the rhythm in the words," and before you know it, we'd be talking about the ancient reconstructed instruments that archaeologists are teaching themselves to play. Have you ever heard an epigonion? If not, you're seriously missing out.

(Just like that. That's exactly how it usually happens.)

"Okay," I say as we pull out of the school parking lot. "I'm not talking about feels. I'm talking about observations here, agreed?"

From behind her blue aviators, Syd cuts me a look. "Agreed."

Twisting my hands around the seat belt, I try to find the right place to start. And there is no right place. I could go all the way back to summer, when we were apart and she got a tattoo without telling me about it. But everything, right now, is an exercise in what-causes-what. I'm going to stick close to home. Immediate.

"I didn't imagine you blowing Hailey off this morning," I say. Facts. Not feels.

The sound Syd makes is nauseating. It's like the gargling of a lugy; after she takes a sharp, clearing inhale through her nostrils. But then, she says, righteously, "We were obviously doing something, and she just sits down."

Also factual but layered with meaning. I acknowledge; I nod. "We were, yeah. But it didn't look like we were doing anything important. I mean, we were sitting there looking at a phone."

"And that cutesy little trick with the face powder," Syd continues. The speedometer rushes above the speed limit, then drops heavily. Cruise control. "Like, does she have dinner with Detective Dad and solve crimes? 'Taco Tuesday? That's for plebes. We have Forensics Friday!'"

I relax. Not because I like what I'm hearing. Just because I kind of understand this. This is a Syd I've met before. When something barbs her skin and drags and irritates until she has to rant it out of her system. And I could see being ticked off that Hailey swept in and solved the problem when Syd was still working on it.

"I'm sorry," I say, but I'm not accepting responsibility. I'm commiserating. "You were this close to getting it."

"Yeah, I was. It would have been cool, too. I was going to breathe on it. Fog the glass."

Syd pulls the lid off her black mittens, exposing her fingers. The pale blue curves of her nails dance along the steering wheel. They move like they're testing the leather, pressing in deep to leave furrows before moving on. Sometimes, she does that to her knee when we're watching movies.

The heat rises quickly in the SUV, and I scramble to turn it down. For some reason, it just feels better to keep an edge of cold on my skin. It soothes me.

"So that's today. But you messed with me about her the first day it snowed."

"I told you it was a joke."

"Right," I say sympathetically. "But I kinda don't believe you."

Syd opens her mouth but says nothing. Instead, she slams on the brakes. The belt across my chest locks, and so do the tires beneath us. We slide on slushy, slick asphalt—rushing up on the bus stopped in front of us. A crush of panic deflates me; I squeeze my eyes closed before impact.

No impact.

We thump back in our seats. I open my eyes, and we're stopped pretty close to a black-and-yellow bumper but only close. We sit high enough off the ground to see the people inside the bus trading seats and talking and carrying on like nothing just happened. For them, I guess, nothing just did.

"Fun," Syd says, shaken.

"Super best mega fun," I reply.

When we move again, Syd doesn't set cruise control. "Look, I don't know why you're so touchy about this—"

"Because you're being a weirdo," I say. Briefly, I consider checking my digital cats. Then I decide that staring at the road nervously will definitely help us arrive safely. "I talk to other people all the time"—not explicitly true—"and I don't get this from you."

Turning things around on me, Syd says, "Okay, well, maybe there's something you want to tell *me*?"

"Like what?"

"Like you *like* her," Syd says. She doesn't have to look over the sunnies. I know she's goggling at me, her own private sideshow. "And you won't admit it. Even to me, and we tell each other everything."

That's what I *thought*, my brain replies. My lips offer up, "I don't know what you're—"

"Oh god, yes you do. If you had seen yourself in the library, you'd be like, 'Ooooh, Syd, that girl is stupid over Hailey Kaplan-Cho.' Heart eyes for *days*. You were knock-kneed and cross-eyed and *so* into her."

My face gets hot. I open the window. "I don't think that's what I looked like."

"And there it is," Syd says, dropping her hand on the gearshift for emphasis. "The denial. How long have I known you?"

"Forever."

"For-ever, Ava. And you're crushing hard and won't even tell me, so what am I supposed to think? Like, does Hailey not like *me* or something?"

"After this morning, probably not."

"Okay, let's not talk about *feels*," Syd says, reflecting me with a slightly hard edge. "Let's just go back to the original question I asked, that you've been cagey about ever since. Do you like her?"

That is *what it is, isn't it?*

I hadn't opened *that* box. That one is marked Pandora and pressed down the deepest. Lying to myself and dancing around it and letting it happen without telling myself what was happening—

Or maybe I don't know what is happening.

Or maybe I know *and* I don't.

"It's complicated," I tell Syd. I'm shocked at how teary I sound. The emotion sprang up on its own; it's too late to smother it. "I think I do? But I don't know how to like a real person. And she hasn't asked about—" I gesture at my face. "Yet. And what if she does? I think it would kill me. But what if she already knows? Her dad's a cop, and he was there. . . ."

Pulling in by the dollar store, Syd drops the car into park. Her sunglasses come off, and there's sympathy behind the tightness of her brow. "And so what? I don't tell people about breaking my arm in fourth grade."

"It's not the same."

"Kind of," Syd announces, turning to me. "Kind of it is. That's not you. That's not, like, the definition of you. It's irrelevant if you want it to be."

God, it's so hot in this car. I roll the window down the rest of the way; I stick my face out of it like a dog. We're not moving, but the cold slaps my cheeks. It fingers down the back of my coat. I need it. I really need it. "It's easy for you to say."

"Because I'm easy?"

She's joking. She tosses it out there like bait; she waits for me to gulp it down.

"You're not afraid," I finally say. "You've made out with people and hooked up and done stuff, and I . . ."

"No, I get it." Unbuckling her seat belt, Syd leans over the console to catch me by the shoulders. "But you're hiding from yourself, Noodle. And lying to yourself and lying to me. And I can't deal with that. I can take anything but that."

The maelstrom in my head quiets, just a bit. The fire recedes, held off by a wide-open window and the cool weight of Syd's gaze on my face. There are things there, other things going on in her head that I can't read or sense or hear.

"We went driving," I say.

Syd slides back to her seat. "And?"

"We held hands."

"And?"

I thought forbidden thoughts about her and asked her to go flying and stared off into the vast winter darkness of the sky. I watched her body cut through weight like a knife, strong-tight-proud. I watched a whole new kind of sunrise in her eyes.

Those I keep to myself. Those rare, precious things. They're too much for words and too private for love songs.

So I admit to Syd and myself and the universe, "I really like her."

But I can't like her. I might be broken. He might have broken me.

Syd flinches. She smiles. Then she says, "Now you wanna tell me what's going on with the bruise?"

THAT SECRET I KEEP. AND IT'S HARD, BECAUSE halfway through a double-cheese light-pepperoni, my phone chirps.

Sprawled out on Syd's bed, I can't even figure out where I put it. I sit up like a startled prairie dog, looking this way, that. Since I'm with Syd, that has to be Mom

(no could be Hailey might be Hailey what if it's Hailey?!)

trying to find out where I am. I should have texted her; I just promised that I would. And I didn't, because Syd wanted to perform an autopsy on every single emotion I've had about Hailey and when things started and what made it happen, and she's just making it so BIG.

Because something feels like it's forming between us, Hailey and me. But it doesn't have an official start yet, does it? Or was my lost glove the start? I have no idea, because the last week of my life has been the most screwed-up one I've ever had. (Since.) Highs and lows, peaks and valleys. All the cacophony in my head makes it hard to pull out single notes.

Especially, *especially*, because I'm leaving out everything about

Jane. My other new friend. My brand-new friend, who's more like me than anyone I've ever met. My friend who walks in the shape of my footsteps, who barely leaves a trace of her own. My friend who understands the way my brain rebels when I'm trying to think private, sexy thoughts. My friend who keenly feels the betrayal of a body when the brain is horrified.

No, I haven't told Syd much about Hailey, and I've told her nothing about Jane, and that's how it is. That's just how it's going to be. Except that's not the way the universe rolls. Syd finds my phone first and reads the notification.

"Who's '1LostMarble at gmail'? That's not Hailey, is it?"

Impaled on the spike of a secret I can't afford to set free, I shake my head. "No, it's my mom. They got mad at her for using her work email for private stuff, so she got a gmail."

Smooth. Smooth like vanilla, like the surface of a duck pond. Smooth like Hailey's wrist. I take my phone from Syd and unlock it. I can pretend this email is from my mom. I can pretend that, no problem. She can't hear the quake in my chest. She doesn't taste the sharp tang in the back of my throat.

Screen open, notification touched. Email takes a second to load. The subject line burns into me like a brand.

SUBJECT: You have my phone.

Rubbing my lips together, I open the message. It's worse, so much worse when I see my own name at the top.

> Ava Parkhurst—
> I want my phone back. Leave it at the customer counter at the Red Stripe in Caribou. Tonight. They close at 11. Don't make me come find you.
> 1LostMarble

A murderer wants his mobile back. A murderer is telling me where he'll be and when. A murderer just gave me everything I need to confront him. Catch him. Keep him from the next Jane, the Jane after next.

(or at least figure out who he is.)

(so I can tell the police?)

(there's a police car in his gallery: to avoid? To escape? Why, why, why?)

(sidenote, dummy: a murderer just threatened you. wake up!)

Something like shock sparks all through me. Adrenaline, like he's right in front of me and I can reach out and grab him.

I will catch him. *I* will be the breakwater he crashes on. I will *not* be the next girl in the woods.

My hands shake faintly; I shove the phone in my pocket. This time, I do need a plan. I didn't mean to run into him in the dark; that's why it went to hell. This is a chance. A specific, deliberate chance. I'm not about to let him track me down. He doesn't get to hunt this time. I'm going to scent him. Take him out.

(somehow)

The Red Stripe is just a little local grocery store. There's nothing special about it. There's no reason to go there specifically, so if

I need a ride there, I need the why.

Why there instead of the Sav-a-Lot? I don't want this to be interesting for Syd. I need her to stay far away from this. But I need her to take me to Caribou. But, but. But.

Jane waits in the dark glass of Syd's window. She could say something here, but she doesn't. Instead, she stares, her eyes sockets and her expression grim. No thumbs-up, no guiding whisper. It's just her, waiting. Full of some kind of expectation. The weight of that presses into me, and I refocus. How. Do. I. Do. This?

Okay.

It's easy to lie to people; it's easy to lie to yourself. It's easy to end up somewhere you shouldn't be. Grocery store in another town; lying on the half shell next to the Aroostook River. If people can't tell when I'm falling apart inside, who says they'll know when I'm plotting?

Syd folds another slice in half, letting the grease drip out on her paper plate before taking a bite. "S'up?"

"Can you drop me at the Red Stripe?" I ask. I try to sound annoyed and distracted. Rubbing a hand against my sleeve, I set off my new tattoo. It burns; it glows like a brand. Things I can't. Things I *can't.* "My mom wants to meet me there."

Syd makes a face. Both incredulous and reasonable, she asks, "Why?"

Like a marionette, I wave my arms too expansively. My head bobbles, exaggerated in its shaking. "I don't even know. That's just what she wants."

"O-kay," Syd says with a shrug. "Did she say when?"

Before eleven is not an answer. That reminds me, I'll need to lie again—to my mother. One at a time, though. Let's just get through this, step by step. Lie first to Syd; lie to Mom next. Hopefully, no more lies. Seems unlikely, but it's organized, anyway. I glance at the clock on my phone and say, "Like, in half an hour?"

"We're gonna have to go, then," Syd says.

"Yeah, sorry," I say.

I am sorry. I really am. She bolts down the rest of that slice; I put on my coat.

Jane doesn't move. She combs her hands through her hair, then twists it into a knot on the top of her head. *I'll meet you there*, her expression says. She knows what I'm going to do. Sometimes, I think she knows everything. Knows me better than I know myself.

We'll see.

SYD DROPPED ME OFF, BUT SHE DIDN'T REALLY WANT TO. Since we didn't see my mom's car when we got there, Syd offered to wait. She pointed out that the tunes in the car were a thousand times better than the Muzak in the store. It was warmer. Cleaner. A little less skeezy.

Caribou is a small town, just like Walker's Corner, but it's big enough to have a good side and a bad side. A comfortable side versus a desperate side. Prime cuts of beef on sale against overpriced chuck roast, $6.99 a pound. The Red Stripe lives in the desperation, and it shows.

Worn, grey—the store looks like it's exhausted. Dingy paint fading in places, the windows marked up with oil-penned, advertised discounts—the store sits in a pot-holed parking lot where only two of the overhead lights work. This is extremely relevant, because it's going to be dark soon.

Uneasy, I considered Syd's offer to stay. I considered telling her about Jane and my non-plan. Syd would have ideas; she'd be passionate and furious. It was possible she could fill in the spaces I'd left empty.

But Jane was mine. Mine to protect, mine to save.

Swearing, promising, insisting that I'd be all right, I finally convinced Syd to drive away. She didn't like it, but the last thing I said was the best lie: a truth that simply wasn't going to happen.

I'm meeting my mom, I'd said. *She's not going to make me wait here long.*

So, reluctantly, Syd left. But you know what? It was nice that she didn't like it. She'd wanted to wait with me, and that felt like a warm fire on a cold night. We'd fixed things; we can sail on toward the horizon without fear.

Really, I don't blame her for being mad at me. I blame her for the way she acted when she was mad, absolutely. But the anger makes total sense. Best friends don't keep secrets from each other. Best friends means keeping secrets *together.* Betrayal ran both ways: I'd felt the same way when I found out she got a tattoo without me.

Wait.

That new tattoo without me. That silent, secret breakup with Meghan.

That happened *before* Hailey.

Before.

On unsteady feet, I push into the store. Skimming past Customer Service, I don't even consider stopping. As if I were really going to just drop off a killer's phone. Not a chance. It's *my* chance to find him. Tail him. Figure out who he is so I can—

There's no end to that sentence. Because I realize, I don't even see it when my best friend is shining me on. In a dance with intricate turns, Syd turned me away from my questions about her.

She'd made it about me. My secrets, my silence. Me.

With deft fingers, she'd plucked out the truth about Hailey. She'd strummed my nerves and made me an instrument to play. Her instrument, played like a symphony over New York slices.

And the whole time, she'd made me feel like *I* was in charge.

Maybe you're surprised I didn't see it.

You shouldn't be, and I'll tell you why.

I rely on routines. I've built my life into this framework of hours. I always go to school. I always hang out with Syd. I always avoid crowds. I never deviate—doing the same thing the same way all the time makes me feel safe. It means I'm in control; nothing happens unless I want it to happen.

Until this very moment, I'm sure that I'm the architect of all things in my current life.

Only it turns out, I'm not.

I didn't plan for Hailey. I didn't expect Jane. I don't know what I'm going to do about 1LostMarble. Everything that seems woven tight unravels. My edges fray; my thoughts tangle. Then I move through a space someone else stood in. It's happened to you: you feel the warmth of their skin on a doorknob or you catch the scent of their perfume.

Here, in the produce, there's asparagus that smells earthy and green, and there's aftershave. Blue, spicy aftershave. The scent crashes into me, an out-of-control train. Everything so orderly, neat, and carefully curated in my head explodes at once.

Unwanted thoughts spill everywhere, and I slip back in time. Back to that summer, to rotting underbrush and hot asphalt and

Aqua Velva. That moment goes on and on; the beginning, the end. The aftermath. Walking home, walking fast, and feeling so *stupid*, so incredibly stupid for talking to a stranger—and angry: at myself. At me, at little me, because I should have somehow known better, and bargaining.

Again, bargaining only with myself: tell no one, say nothing, and it will all go away (*except you deserve it, if it doesn't all go away*). Crying, dirty, ashamed—trying to hide what he did to me: I feel that all the way down in my gut. It's all real again; it's *now*.

It's raw nerve instead of careful detail spreading over me. There's the ugly, heavy weight lower than my stomach, lower than my navel. Invasion. Violation. Hot, mint breath in my face. The sweet, shocking notes of leather, of aftershave.

Sensation has no edge, and emotion is every color. And this time, Jane doesn't rescue me. She doesn't whisper, "It's fine." Her face doesn't float up in the gleam of chrome shelves.

On my own, I have to shake there and swallow the bile in my throat. I have to hold oranges. I have to watch the Customer Service counter without really seeing. I have to wait for my body horror to work itself out and climb back in its box.

Shuddering, I put the orange down. When the past loses its grip, it's time to scrape my skin clean again. To bleach my brain and remind myself, *not my fault, not damaged, not used up, not spoiled*.

I push my cart. I sharpen my gaze and stare at the Customer Service corral deliberately. 1LostMarble is going to show up and ask for his phone. I'm going to follow him. I'm going to put this down.

Because I survived. I got to go home; I got to build my walls and cages and keep going. I get to have moments that aren't about this one, terrible thing. Yes, it comes back. It sneaks up and spoils me again, but there are times without.

Jane will never get to have the times without. Her worst day is her last day. All she'll be is the way she died. To everyone but me, she'll just be a body.

(Body Found Near Aroostook River

Police Investigating Body Found in Shallow Grave

Body of Murdered Woman Still Unidentified

Homicide Detectives Find Few Clues about Dumped Body)

Picking up a pear, I ponder its mottled green surface, then raise it to my nose. It smells sweet, at the edge of sickly. The flesh is soft; it's ripe today, but tomorrow, rotten. And yes, I see how that applies. I do see it.

I do realize

(basket case)

what I'm doing is probably not *ideal* and probably wrong and mixed up and muddled, and I don't even have an end point in sight. I get that. I do.

But I also know if I had given Jane up when I found her, I wouldn't be thisclose to catching her killer in Caribou. I never even *go* to Caribou. I literally wouldn't be here without that decision. Without Syd acting weird, without my needing a tattoo.

It's like my history teacher parsing out when the "American experiment" began. If Richard III hadn't murdered two kids to steal the English crown, then barely royal, on-the-wrong-side-of-the-family Henry Tudor would have never had a claim to the throne.

Without Henry Tudor taking up the crown at Bosworth Field, no Tudor heirs. No Henry VII means no Henry VIII, and thus, without Anne Boleyn, no Protestant revolution in England. Without a Protestant revolution in England, no Puritans, so bibbidi-bobbidi-boo, Richard III did, in fact, kick off the American experiment.

(There are so many other ways it could have happened, but it didn't.)

So I *had* to find Jane. I *had* to keep her. And now I *have* to wait here, in this grocery store, under grey flickering lights, watching for the boy who killed her. And then I have to—

Do something.

That part of my plan remains fuzzy. What am I going to do? Gather evidence, maybe? Make the case? Who am I, Sherlock Holmes? I don't know the first thing about investigating a murder. All I see is the end goal: he doesn't *get away* with murder.

He doesn't get to *keep* Jane. He finds out what it's like to be stolen away from *his* life, to lose everything. To suffer.

But, again, it's that middle piece I'm missing. My stomach roils at the prospect of giving Jane up to the police. They'll touch her, cut her, break her down like she's a deer, and throw all her insides back inside her when they're done. They'll defile her and pretend it's for a good reason.

If I give them her killer before I give them her body, they might skip that part. I think? I don't *know*.

God, what have I gotten myself into?

THE RED STRIPE SINKS INTO ITS OWN DEPRESSION AS night spills down around it. The people who come through the single working door are exhausted. Shadows leave smudges beneath their eyes; they walk with weary gazes and weights on their feet.

They come in wearing uniforms for other grocery stores, for McDonaldses, for pharmacies. Sometimes alone, sometimes with kids. The kids mostly sit in the carts, high enough to see and cry for all the things they want, loud as alarms when their parents buy staples instead of sugar cereal.

All these people, with their own troubles, their own lives, come and go. They select frozen pizzas and rotisserie chickens, instant mashed potatoes and thigh quarters, only sixty-nine cents a pound.

The employees congregate at the front of the store. A guy in an orange safety vest drives trains of carts into the corral, then stops at Customer Service whenever the cashier drifts away from her register for a chat.

The cashier's noticed me, for sure, because every time she comes back to her aisle, she looks me over with a deepening frown.

It's not illegal to browse but okay.

Gliding on to frozen foods, the second-best view of the front of the store, I check my phone again. No new email. Just the one, demanding swift return of the cell in my possession . . . or else.

An overhead speaker crackles to life. "We will be closing in twenty minutes. Please make your final selections. Thank you for shopping Red Stripe."

Twenty minutes, and he still hasn't shown. He wanted it bad enough to give me a place, to give me a time, but he's not here yet. Why isn't he here yet? Even if he's one of those always-late people who call and say, "Almost there," when they're still in their towel after a shower, he picked a time! A place! And threatened to find *me* if I skip out, so where is he?

He killed someone and I have all the evidence, but it's not, like, urgent to him? I could have turned up at 10:58 or 7:14, and yet he's not checking the counter? He doesn't come up, again and again, asking, "Did somebody find my phone? Did somebody turn it in?"

I've been around and around this store, and fact: he's not skulking in the produce. He's not watching the counter, waiting for me to appear. There are no repeats, no lingerers, no twitchy guys in hoodies swooping in through the automatic door.

So, what, then? He's just okay with his phone full of semi-evidence sitting in a drawer until he gets around to picking it up? He's going to wait until tomorrow to retrieve his precious? I don't think he's a lot older than me; he should probably be in school tomorrow.

(THEN AGAIN, *when trying to retrieve evidence that you murdered a girl and left her buried in the snow, possibly, just perhaps,* TRUANCY *is not actually an issue, Ava.)*

My cart squeaks as I skim along cases of frozen pizzas. I feel more and more obvious by the moment. Is there a chance, is it possible, that *he's* watching *me*? That the phone was bait, which I swallowed. He's already killed one girl. He could have already picked out my grave.

No. That's crazy.

I have his phone, and he needs it back. There's guilt on it. Evidence in it. I may not understand the gambit, but I really do think he needs it all back. He could have already deleted it remotely, and he hasn't. He wants what he's got left on there; it is a prize. It is *important.*

As the clock ticks toward eleven, my chest tightens. If he's going to show up, now would be the time. The man behind the deli counter turns out the lights. The Muzak overhead abruptly cuts off at a quarter till. It's not like it was good music, but its absence is eerie.

Now I hear other carts moving, out of sight. Cases opening. Bags rustling. An irrational, giddy part of my brain points out how much this feels like a zombie movie . . . right before the zombies attack.

God, brain, just shut up. There are no zombies, and this guy is *not* going to show. Not today, and I can't set up camp in a grocery store until he does.

At random, toss a couple of frozen pizzas into my cart. They look absurd, huddling in the corner without anything else around them. I feel suspicious and obvious and wildly out of place. Somehow, buying something will make that better.

Just in case, I grab two bags of Doritos on my way to check out, too. There. That's better. Four whole things, to justify how long I spent wandering.

"You have a Red Stripe card?" the clerk asks by rote.

I shake my head no. I stand, poised at the card reader, with my phone. When the total comes up, I touch my phone to the reader and nothing happens. With a frown, I touch it again.

"Oh," the clerk says flatly. "We don't have one of those. You have to put your card in."

"Oh," I echo, embarrassed.

I hope I have my card. It's probably stuck behind my school ID, in a wallet that perpetually sinks to the bottom of my bag. It's a two-arm expedition to get down there, shoving aside the remains of recent snacks.

Empty animal cracker bags, half-full party mix bags (I eat only the brown chippy things), two unopened bags of Takis Fuego . . . Why do I have so much food with me? Loose change and Starburst, tubes of Carmex and Chapstick—

"Bringing in the carts."

My spine snaps straight. It's that *voice.* That mechanical, almost human voice I found on the killer's phone.

It's *him.*

I KEEP DIGGING, SLOWER NOW, AND LOOK OVER MY shoulder.

It's the bag boy, the cart guy, whatever, who's been coming and going all night. He stands by the Customer Service counter, his arms folded on top of it.

Between his hands, a phone—he texts someone with swift thumbs. Only, when he hits Send, that digital voice speaks again. "There's one across the street again. I'm gonna leave it there."

The automatic door opens; cold sweeps in. Sweeps over me, steals my breath.

All this time, I've been waiting for this guy to skulk in and ask for his phone. Someone from the outside, with shifty eyes and a dark aura or something. Black clothes and menace incarnate.

And that's stupid. That's so stupid.

Monsters and murderers and rapists and fiends aren't slavering, bug-eyed creatures from central casting. I know that better than anybody. Nobody willingly goes off with a snaggle-toothed, unwashed demon of a man.

Monsters are charming. They're pleasant. They ask if you want to see—

"Girlie?" the cashier says expectantly.

Down into my bag again, I find and drop, drop and find my wallet. It takes me a moment to remember my PIN. Hands trembling, hips aching to run, I manage to type in 1066

(the Battle of Hastings; William the Conqueror slaughters Harold Godwinson; au revoir, Anglo-Saxons; bonjour, Normans)

on the second try. Beepity, approved, thanks for shopping at Red Stripe, thanks, have a nice night.

Even as I take a step, I stare. He's there. He's *right there*; been there all night, in and out, before my eyes. The red smock had made him invisible—I didn't see; how lucky am I that he didn't, either?

He slides his other phone into his back pocket and heads outside again.

I follow. The cold engulfs me, instantly piercing me in every direction. It's colder at the far, dark corner of the building, but it's a better view. When he trudges into the side lot and stalks back to the front—he's right there, never out of sight. With frigid fingers, I fumble with my phone, trying to wake it.

It's my turn to stalk, to take photos without permission.

Unlike him, however, I remember to turn off the flash. From every possible angle, I steal his image.

Battering one cart into another, he builds a stainless-steel snake. That takes strength. The line of carts grows, but he controls them. They don't veer or stick in the slush and packed-down ice in the parking lot. His face is concentration: brows furrowed, lips pursed.

Right there are the hands that beat Jane Doe. There is the last face she ever saw in this life. There's the man—the *boy*—who took everything from her and still wants more.

"Bet you want to hit him," Jane says, murmuring right in my ear. Her voice shocks me. I feel her breath on my neck. Feel the anger in her skin.

When I glance back, Jane's an ice-white phantom. Bloodless. Gouged. Face swollen; eye disappearing behind a bloody clot of red and purple. She puts her hand on my shoulder—no fingertips. Her fingers are nubs that brand my skin, right through my coat.

I know it's not right, that she's not real—

(basket case)

But she is. She's my fraternal twin. My worst-case scenario, closed up in a tree and blanketed only by snow. Jane's a better friend to me than Syd; Jane's not conflicted. She doesn't change the subject.

"You probably shouldn't," Jane whispers. She rests her misshapen head on my shoulder. "But I know you want to."

And it's scary because yeah, I do. I want to hit him. I want to *hurt* him, tear him to pieces, break his bones, split his skull—

I close my eyes and fight back the urge. Nice girls shouldn't get angry. They shouldn't explode. They don't raise their voices, make a scene, lash out. But tamping down my feelings—it's like trying to stop a magma flow. Anger and rage flow over obstacles and then consume them.

Right now, I'm *not* a nice girl.

And I'm not as subtle as I thought I was, either.

He looks up at me as I raise my phone to take a picture. He stares at me in double—thirty yards away in the flesh, thirty inches away in twelve megapixels on the screen. My lungs tighten; chest hitching, I drop the phone to my side and pretend I was taking a selfie or something. That's normal; selfies in a dark parking lot in ten-degree weather at 11:08 p.m.

Our connection is a guitar string strung tight. It quivers, waiting for a touch. And then he plucks it.

"H-hhhey!" he yells. Abandoning the carts, he starts for me. Head down, shoulders broad, face furious. Steam spills out of his nostrils. His eyes burn, and I already know he's fast.

I'm faster.

I run.

I DON'T KNOW CARIBOU; CARIBOU DOESN'T KNOW ME.

When I bolt through a back alley, I crash into dark trash cans. Not the metal kind. The giant plastic ones that you lock. (You can't be too careful when you live this close to wilderness. Dogs, cats, raccoons, rats, and bears! Right there in your backyard! And bears, my friends, can open back doors and car doors, so yeah. Don't teach them to eat where you live.)

I stumble-leap over the cans, but lights come on in the houses around me. It feels like new eyes fall on me. Strangers watching. They should. I'm not dangerous, but I *could* be. Pay attention, people. Pay attention!

Somebody shoveled between the narrow fences; put down some salt, too. Everything back here is running through dark grey mush. It soaks through my boots; it'll freeze on them, too. A dark pile rises in front of me. No idea what that is. Jump!

Something wrenches in my back. I land hard. Skid. Fire shoots down my hip, but I don't stop.

Footsteps slosh behind me. I don't look back because that's how you die in horror movies. I know who's chasing me. I know what happens if he catches me. A sickly orange streetlight illuminates the end of the alley. I am its earthbound moth. We are all that exists: me, that light.

Two words clang in my head. Reckless. Stupid. Reckless. Stupid. They make me run faster. Left foot is Stupid; right foot is Reckless. They pound and splash. My heart beats in time. My breath is fire, scorching my throat, searing my lungs.

Skidding out of the alley, I turn Stupid, deeper into the knot of houses just off the highway. Recklessward is woods, and I know I can't run in there. The white noise of escape fills my head. I have my beat, stupid-reckless, and now a static haze fills out the melody.

It's like I'm alone. I'm not outrunning the devil, just myself. I'm beating my own time. From the outside, I probably look insane. I run right down the middle of the side streets. The sidewalks are still covered in snow. I flicker beneath halogen lights; I don't stop for stop signs.

Inside, I'm molten—for a few timeless, perfect moments, I'm high. Untouchable. Immaculate.

Then it all crashes. From the inside, not the out. My stamina drops. My muscles melt. Strength spills from me, and it hurts to breathe. All the thoughts that were so clear turn to grey haze. *Where am I going? What was I doing?*

I'm a wobbly, rubbery dolly. I stagger into the middle of an intersection before stumbling to a stop. Everything in my bloodstream is wrong. The cold hits hard. My stomach clenches, and I have to grab my own knees to keep my balance. There's a high-pitched ringing in my ears, and I can barely find the fortitude to raise my head.

Four stop signs waver in the wind. The roads are narrow here, no lines. And empty. Swaying, I veer around to double-check that. Empty, empty; I'm alone.

In the dark.

In a strange town.

Because I followed a killer.

My body is heavy now. The call and answer of stupid-reckless isn't sharp anymore. It's a corrupted MP3, warbling and scratched with electronic spikes. A muddled mix of pain wells inside me. I just stand there. Right there, in the middle of the intersection, with no idea what to do next.

A cheerful ping startles me. My phone, still clutched tight in my hand. It's like I'm moving through molasses now (maybe this is one of those nightmares?), but I finally clear the lockscreen and raise it to my face. A bluish glow washes over me. It feels so good; so safe.

Where are you? my mother demands.

A burst of emotion threatens to overwhelm me. I want to tell her, *I don't know, and I'm scared, and come save me.* I want to tell her, *It's dark out, I'm cold, I'm somewhere in Caribou.* I want to beg her to make everything all right.

Instead, I reply with shaky hands, Hanging out with Syd. I told you I was going to.

That was hours ago, she types furiously. Do you know what time it is?!

Headlights rise in the distance, and I step out of the street. I need to figure out what I'm going to do here, sooner rather than later. People will eventually notice a stranger standing outside their houses in the middle of the night.

Sorry!! I text.

••• hovers there, three-eyed monster in the dark. Then comes her reply. Forewarning next time!

Yes. Next time I go to Caribou to stalk a murderer, I will definitely tell Mom first. Maybe she can pack me a dinner bag, tuna salad sandwiches, no crusts. Goldfish. A juice box. I haven't even started my reply when Mom texts again.

I'm not kidding! I need to know where you are! All times!

A whole bramble of barbed wire tightens in my chest. Her exclamation points are the sharpest points, piercing deep. I'm seventeen, and historically responsible and level headed. I have a phone; I know how to call for help if I need it.

(Okay, I don't do it, but I know how.)

(I would if I really needed to.)

(Probably.)

So what is going on? Are you staying the night or what?!

Well, I can't call Syd without a lot of explanation—she thinks I met my mom. And I can't ask Mom to come get me, because she's throwing an epic wobbly because I'm not already home. The ground scrapes beneath my boots as I turn, calculating my next destination.

Yes, I tell Mom.

According to the map on my phone, my Lyft will arrive in fourteen minutes.

IN BOOKS AND MOVIES, THERE ARE ALWAYS convenient trees and trellises outside second-story windows. Pebbles, too, plenty of them lying around. Just the right size to toss at a window. Not too big, can't break the glass, but just big enough to make a noise.

Standing beneath a naked maple tree in Hailey's front yard, I realize I don't even know which window is hers. So I won't be climbing, and I definitely won't be doing any geological window tapping. Instead, I text her and watch the house avidly.

You up?

Yeah. What's up?

Good question. It has too many answers, so I deflect. Look out the front window.

A moment passes, and then the curtains part in one of the upstairs windows. What little light there is comes from behind, so I only see the shape of her. But I know it's her, with her wild, flyaway hair and arms made of velvet and steel. The curve of her shoulders in silhouette entrances me.

Raising a hand, I wait for her to see me. I thumb directions into my phone. Under the tree.

Her posture sharpens and she replies, Omg what are you doing out there?

Can I come in?

There's a pause before she answers. Come around to the back door.

Like a burglar, I steal into her backyard. The gate protests when I open it; it's so loud. I expect everyone in the neighborhood to stick their heads out their windows. If the gate doesn't do it, the crunch of snow will. My every footstep cracks through the icy shell on top of tall drifts. I'm a suburban yeti out here; somebody's gonna notice.

Somehow, I get to the back door. It's open just a crack, and Hailey peers through it. When she sees me, she pushes it open in an elaborate ballet. A push, a twirl, strands of her hair floating softly in the wind.

Holding open the storm door, she presses her back to the inner door and waits for me to slip inside. I brush against her: coated, scarfed, booted. She's just wearing sleep shorts and a T-shirt.

"Cold," Hailey whispers.

I whisper back, "I know, right?"

When I get past her, she closes up carefully. A soft chirp confirms the alarm. No doors slam; no locks creak. The house is quiet, warmed with the hum of the furnace and contained by the ticking of a clock. Hailey doesn't have to shush me. I take her hand when she offers it.

Thick, sweet floral perfume hangs in the air. An air freshener in the key of lilac or lavender; I always forget which one is which. As she leads me down the hall and up the stairs, I try to drink in all the details of her house. What little I see as we sneak toward her room paints a picture.

A slightly cluttered, lived-in picture: cool leather couches with warm winter afghans thrown over the backs. Curtains that match; family photos alternating with pretty landscape photography.

Books, paper, mail stacked on a table by the door; a coatrack laden with jackets and scarves and umbrellas. That makes me smile: the sight of umbrellas hanging from the hooks. Her house is nothing like mine.

When we get to Hailey's room, she shuts the door tight and locks it. Lush, rich colors surround me: purples and reds and oranges. Her room feels like a fantasy: shelves full of books and sports trophies, a glittery bead curtain hanging over the window, oversized pouf chairs on the floor.

Every flat surface is covered in a crazy jumble of her life. A single shin guard lays on her dresser full of jewelry, and Hufflepuff schwag pops up everywhere: a tie dangles from the side of her mirror; three different badger stickers adorn her headboard.

Seeming happily baffled, Hailey asks, "What are you doing here?"

"It's been a long weird night, and I just wanted to see you." Then I feel a shade of guilt that's not nearly dark enough. I offer something that's not really an apology, because I'm really hoping she doesn't mind the intrusion. "I don't want to get you in trouble."

She laughs. "It's fine. Dad's on nights, and Mom's on Xanax."

"Then why did I come in the back door?"

"Because the neighbors are really, really nosy."

At that, I laugh. Sneaking in for the sake of sneaking in, after turning up in the middle of the night—this is turning into a good adventure. A journal story, one of the ones I might talk about for fun when I'm thirty and average and stuff.

"Okay, so," she says, then pushes off the door. At first, I think she's going to hug me, the way she comes toward me. I'm tight, then I soften when she grabs my lapels. Tugging my zipper, she smiles. "You should take off your coat and stay awhile."

There's a bolt when our hands touch. Static electricity, but it feels monumental. Our hands weave and dodge as she helps me from my coat. Every glancing brush of her skin against mine is a drug. It burns away the cold and sets me on a dreamy, drunken kind of path.

The bad fades because she's standing so close. The wait in the Red Stripe, the chase—packed away for another time. I'm not standing here, deaf and dumb in front of the prettiest girl I know and pretending I just came here to talk.

I shrug my coat the rest of the way off. It falls heavily at my feet. Hands finally free, I actually skim them against her waist.

(I'm touching her! I'm touching her!)

One cold ring finger grazes against her skin where her shirt rode up. She shivers and presses in. Dark strands of her hair drift toward me, electrically charged. One makes contact; I shiver.

She pulls off my scarf, and the fabric crackles on my neck. Her laughter is soft, and she murmurs, "Ow."

"Seriously, ow," I say back.

The room is small and tight around us. It gets tighter when

Hailey folds her arms and insinuates her fingers against me. Right against my ribs; they slot right into the spaces. Even though I'm still fully dressed, I feel stripped against her. My body forgets how to breathe. It forgets how to be.

It forgets how to be afraid, just for a moment.

When I kiss her, our lips cling together. They're not tentative or afraid—they long to hold on to the soft, silken glow between us. Her lips seek when I falter. They're plush and they invite me in.

She teaches me with a taste how to follow. I've never done this before. Every flicker is terrifying and exhilarating; it's the first leap off the high dive and cutting flawlessly into the water. Twisting my hands in her shirt, my knuckles rasp against forbidden skin.

Hailey unfurls against me. When she twines her arms around me, her blunt nails skate the length of my spine. They brush aside the hem of my shirt and whisper at the small of my back. It's alchemy, drinking something that makes us grow and grow, fill up the room and spill out of it, into the universe.

It's so much, too much, and we break away at the same time. I burrow against her; she holds me tighter.

"Hi," I say.

I feel her smile on my skin.

IT'S HARD TO GET SOMETHING YOU DON'T EXPECT.

Something that you should probably want—okay, something I *want* but wasn't *ready* to want. This is the problem with going off the rails and chasing demons and angels in the dark. I'm not planning; I'm only reacting. And only reacting is—

I've shared a bed with Syd before, so I'm like, *I can handle sharing Hailey's.* Lying to myself, like it's just going to be sleeping; it's not. But it's also not sex. Just kissing, just close, just skin-on-skin with clothes between, just breath hot on my lips and hands heavy on my hips.

And when Hailey offers, it's like, *Yeah, we're going to sleep. Just sleeping here. No big deal.*

First, she lends me a T-shirt and shorts to sleep in. They're a little tight, and they smell just like her. I'm literally wrapped in her, and then I slide between covers with her, and lay my head on her pillows, and lace my fingers with hers, and I'm *drowning.*

Then we curl face to face. Her smooth legs swim against mine; our brows rest together. I feel like I'm inside her skin or she's inside mine. Sweat springs up between my breasts and along my spine.

Even her voice is physical, velvet stroked along every nerve in the dark.

"You have so many tattoos," she says. She hesitates, then brushes a finger against the mini elephant (Shawn Mendes) a few inches beneath my collarbone. "I never realized."

"I have to hide them from my mom."

She traces the lines of the elephant—she's on forbidden skin and it makes me shiver. "Does it hurt?"

"Yes." I strum my fingers against her arm. My head spins; I float free and swirl back down against her. She catches my foot between her ankles. I'm a desperate tangle of want. The problem is, the craving is formless. It's a hunger; I want all of her, and I have no idea what to do with her.

Hailey traces the other side of my collarbone, where the skin is plain and undecorated. "How many do you have?"

I can't count right now. I can't even think. "A lot."

"My mother would kill me if I got one."

"Mine would too," I say, and grin. "You and Syd are the only ones who know about them."

"So I'm your secret-keeper," she says. She's not looking in my eyes; her gaze falls somewhere around my mouth. My lips sting, and she's not even touching them. And that makes me wonder why not.

Why not and *Things I Can* and all that shapeless desire give me a push. A little clumsily, I steal a kiss. Just a little one, but it makes us both sigh.

When Hailey raises her eyes to mine again, she murmurs, "I've never had an illicit sleepover before."

"Really?"

"Are you surprised?"

"No," I say. I'm not. How could I be? "I haven't either, so, you know, it's nice. More than nice."

It's her turn to graze a kiss on my mouth. She lingers longer, surer. She even knows how to bump and nudge so I fit better against her. I'm falling fast, infatuated with all her little details. Her cleverness, her warmth—the way she feels when she blushes, but I can't make out the shade on her cheeks in the dark.

"That's all I want," she says. "To be more than nice."

And then she bends my arm. Gently—everything about her here is gentle. But she bends it and folds it, sort of, and somehow—I'm not sure how—she tucks it against me. Sort of beneath. Sort of trapped while she dips her fingers free and then knots them again in mine. Her pinkie was on the inside; now it's out. Now her weight shifts against me

(no no no)

and she presses me against the bed, but not really against the bed, and look. The words aren't there. The words are a list of ingredients. They're bone dry and bitter, and they vaguely represent what's happening. But they're not the *feel* of it. The soul of it. And the soul of it is, for two seconds, maybe three, I'm just not in Hailey's bed anymore.

It's summer, and sunshine. And blue sky above, and trees that curve over my head, and toward the apartments. People have windows open. Music filters out, but I don't know the song. I'm glad I don't know the song,

(what is it what is it I bet you can remember if you try try hard Ava go on try and remember THAT

SONG)

and I'm sorry my eyes are open, because it's a nice day, a beautiful day, the best day, hottest all summer, and he's *holding me down* with his pinkie on the outside and my arms folded under me. I'm a broken baby bird, cupped in dirty hands that stain me and make it impossible to go back to the nest. He's on me now; he'll always be on me.

(*this is probably why your dad bailed*)

(And all this happened eight years ago, but it's happening now, all over again. All of it, beginning to end, all summer in a *day*, you guys, *all summer in a day*.)

And Hailey eclipses the sun and asks, worried, "Ava?"

I'm so stiff. My breath is so thin. My brains roll around like loose marbles in my head, clacking and snapping together as they try to make a thought. Beneath the thin cotton of Hailey's T-shirt, my heart pounds—not infatuation. Adrenaline. Fight or flight or, in this case, freeze. I froze and I'm frozen and I don't even know how to tell her what's wrong.

"Are you okay?" Hailey asks. Now she's afraid and maybe hurt and obviously confused.

I shake my hand a little until she lets go. If my pinkie is on the outside, it's okay. That's a rule. One I just learned, so it's not my fault I didn't warn her. This moment is a helium balloon with a cruel clown face on it, and I want to let it float away.

"Just not . . . like that," I say, and lunge to grab her hand again. "Okay?"

"Okay," she says. Uncertain; she doesn't understand.

So I kiss her, and her mouth is sweet and good and tender. Mine is stiff and clumsy. It's not the same now, and so I breathe and she breathes, and I change the subject. I press closer. I squeeze her hand tighter. I rub my nose against hers, and I ask how many times she sorted into Hufflepuff, because it's cute and safe and light.

It's like I'm apologizing with my body for my body. I am my own secret that I don't want to tell.

IN MY DREAMS, JANE STUMBLES THROUGH THE forest.

She's a gothic heroine: white gown, black hair tangled by the wind, barefoot. Everything is black and white: white snow, black trees, white skin, bruises black like dahlias. The river is a black ribbon unspooling; it matches the one tied tight around her neck.

So the blood is a shock. A single poppy blooming on the gown. Jane digs her fingernails into her face and drags. Furrows follow her touch; they well up with scarlet beads. The wind shifts. Her hair flies forward, impossibly forward. Strands stick in the blood, and Jane collapses to her knees.

With raw hands, she digs into the snow. White drifts turn pink; black earth collects beneath her nails. There's something here, something under. Her shoulder blades cut the back of the gown as she works. They protrude: clipped, vestigial wings that will spread.

Temperature dropping, Jane breathes hard, but no steam rises from her lips. She looks back at me, her eyes white and clouded. Splits open in her skin; yellow fat bubbles out. She's strange stained glass; I catch glimpses of her bones beneath. Slowly she raises one hand, like she's going to wave to me.

Her fingertips fall off, one by one.

That's when I realize it's a dream. When I know I'm asleep. That knowing is a trap, though. I want to wake up, but I can't. I'm not sure why. Pressing my back to a tree, I try to warn Jane that she's losing her insides and her outs. Air, forced into my throat, refuses to rise to sound. My lips move, but I have no voice.

Heaving herself to her feet, Jane lurches toward me. She's a puppet on a string. Floating just above the ground, her toes drag grooves in the snow as she makes her way to me. There's nothing in her masked eyes, but she reaches for me all the same.

My voice still won't come. A weight crushes my breastbone. If it breaks, I'm sure, absolutely sure, that my ribs will break. They'll pierce my flesh from the inside out, rising white and sharp and spindly from the black.

"Hey," Jane says, reaching for me. "Let's hold hands."

Her stunted fingers close over mine. She forces my pinkie inside and leans in. Anticipation is a poisonous mix of hope and horror. It's bright and bitter and green, slipping through my veins as Jane sways close. Her lips are ice, brushing my cheek. She leans so close, I feel her lashes on my temple, her nose against my cheek.

Finally, the dam in my throat breaks. I say, "What are we doing?"

Jane's grip tightens. The stubs of her fingers dig between the tendons in my hand. If she doesn't let go, they're going to split my skin and peel my fingers apart like a fried onion. "Whatever you want. I'll do anything you want."

I'm frozen.

"What do you want?" Jane asks. Her tongue is thick in her mouth now. New splashes of blood spread on the canvas of her face.

My bones snap in her grip, and I whimper. I don't pull away; why don't I pull away? "You're hurting me."

"You're hurting me," she agrees.

She doesn't let go. I don't move. A siren wails, and a murder of crows explodes into flight above us. They're black on the grey sky. They fly; they escape. They're gone, and all that's left is the sound of my breath and the crack of my bones. It's just the two of us in this expanse.

Alone.

Except there's a hand on my back. One that's alive. One that's warm; it strokes along my spine with a sweet, luring touch. A voice seeps in, and the woods burn away to darkness.

"Hey," Hailey says again. This time she strokes my shoulder and presses her face close to mine. "Wake up. Ava, wake up. You're having a bad dream."

Even though I open my eyes, it's still dark. I'm aware enough to be embarrassed, and I raise a hand. It skates against Hailey's arm, and I say, "I'm sorry."

"It's okay." When she leans over me, her hair falls like a curtain. It hides us, cutting off the rest of the world in a fragrant cloud. "You just sounded scared."

"I'm okay," I say.

"Okay," she says. Then she slips closer and kisses me. She kisses me again and again, and it never ends. We drift back into sleep: laced, tangled, knitted, one. I don't dream after that.

I don't need to.

I WEAR MY JEANS AND ONE OF HAILEY'S SWEATERS to school.

It's the sweetest kind of torment. She's wrapped around me, her scent setting off fireworks at unexpected intervals. The knit is buttery soft, and it makes my healing tattoos itch. It's a constant reminder that I kissed the girl, and the girl kissed me.

It's a rising tide inside me, a hundred-year flood, and I love the way it makes me float. Sailing down the history hallway, I smile when people pass me. Do I look giddy? Then I look giddy, because I feel it. We held hands in the car; we kissed when we had to walk in two different directions.

This must be the thing that Syd chases. Intellectually, I've understood that crushes and kisses are wonderful/terrible, but I didn't *get* it. Now this—no wonder she buys a ticket to this carnival. No wonder she wants it again and again; the rides leave you dizzy, and everything tastes so sweet.

I slide into Mr. Burkhart's class, and say *hello, hello, hello* to all the people I know. One of the girls laughs. Not at me. With me, like, my smile roused her smile, and it's a moment. The lights are brighter today, hearts lighter. I am Mary Freaking Poppins right now, and I don't even care.

Splashing into my seat, I scrub my fingers through my hair to toss it carelessly. I didn't get to blow it dry this morning, so I'm a little poufy. Hailey and I got ready separately, and we both had to hurry. We had a window between her mom leaving for work and her dad getting home, and we had to hit it hard.

It was a game. And Hailey's mouth is so soft after a hot shower. Shockingly soft, enough to make me wish we were the skipping school types.

As I sit in my desk in Mr. Burkhart's class, I do that stupid movie thing. I touch my lips, remembering the weight of Hailey's there. My heart beats on a strange loop; it's like it's loose inside me and leaping for joy.

My phone chirps, and I swipe it open.

Want to hear something crazy? Hailey texts.

Another loop for my heart. I type back, Always. I love crazy.

I'm seriously sitting here wondering if it's possible to skip school if you're already here.

LOL, I reply. I was thinking the same thing. Here's my crazy. I already miss you.

Miss you too, she says, and follows it up with the blushy emoji.

Ugh, god, I feel like I'm going to explode. There's too much inside me for my skin to contain. Sprawling on my desk, I hold my phone in front of me and somehow get the nerve to send back the kissy smiley.

Everything with Hailey is fast; the right kind of fast. The kind of speed you want to try to keep up with; it's the running of the bulls, the Indy 500. And tonight, we're going flying again. Has anyone ever died from anticipation? Because it feels like I might. It feels like I *want* to. Except then I have to resurrect myself, because I don't want to miss out on her.

Hey do you want a ride in the mornings? I can pick you up.

!!!!! I text. Definitely. Yes. Please.

Hailey sends back a shower of hearts, some stars, several rainbows, and the party horn. The emojis fill the screen. Digital confetti, bright and bold and super hyped. They're perfect, better than words. They say everything, and I literally drop my head on my desk and squeak.

I'm ridiculous, I'm wonderful, I'm shackled so hard.

I can't wait to see her again.

"WHAT ARE YOU ON?"

Syd shakes her head at me as, together, we knife down the hallway. Sometime between dropping me off at the Red Stripe yesterday and second block today she added deep purple tips to her blue curls. She's iridescent, some glistening siren set free to entrance the sorry souls that inhabit Aroostook North High School. Poor things, they never had a chance.

I tug my bag onto my shoulder. "Nothing. A cinnamon latte."

"No," she says, bumping me to steer me around a puddle on the floor. "Cinnamon latte doesn't make you *giggly.*"

Without warning, I burn up with a smile. It's not even on purpose. It just happens: smiles and happy sighs escaping all by themselves. I want to spill it, a pitcher overturned and flooding everywhere. I got my first kiss

(first chosen kiss)

and my second and my third. I felt want with somebody, with an actual human person who wanted me back. Hailey's perfume engulfs me, and it's just right there. Right there: I could tell Syd how Hailey woke me up from a nightmare, how she looked in morning darkness, like the sun waiting to rise.

A silent alarm trips in my head, though. *Slow down! Think! Remember! Syd played all around the subject of Hailey. Tread carefully. Move wisely.*

I think I choose my words judiciously. "I don't know. Things with Hailey . . ."

Let her finish the sentence. Multiple choice: Are good. Are progressing. Heated up. All of the above.

Syd writes in a selection of her own. Knowingly, amused, she asks, "Are you guys sexting?"

"No!"

She seems taken aback to have guessed wrong. "Then what?"

I draw the deepest breath. I hold it. The ache feels so good in my lungs, and I glitter again when I let it out, air and truth. "We kissed."

What I expect: Syd to be shocked but delighted. Possibly scandalized. Hungry for details and insistent that she get all of them. What I get is the crackle of brand-new ice. She frosts over, instantly, completely. Her pale eyes fix in the distance. "When?"

"Last night," I say. I tremble in a place between fragile and furious. I want her excitement. I want what she got from *me* when she turned in her kissginity at the lake in middle school. I leapt at her feet and lapped up the details like a dog; like a dog, I was almost happier for her than she was for herself.

There's stone beneath Syd's ice now. She looks at me, hard. "*When* last night?"

"Last night-last night," I tell her. "After you dropped me off."

"I thought you had to meet your mom."

I hadn't forgotten that lie. I don't trip over it. "I did. And we went home, and then I went over to Hailey's."

Suddenly, Syd barks a laugh. It's all incredulity and annoyance as she veers into the wall and stops. "Seriously?"

"Seriously!"

"How stupid do I look?" she demands. "You bailed on me, and you made me give you a ride to do it! God, I knew you were full of it. The Red Stripe? Seriously?!"

Long, hard zaps of anxiety rush from my spine into the back of my head. I don't want to fight in front of the school—I don't want to fight at all. But if we have to, it should be private.

This is exposure; this is armor off and vulnerable skin, and I don't want—*can't*—feel this way at school. I keep my voice low and say, "I didn't meet Hailey in Caribou. I met up with her after. It was the middle of the night!"

Syd doesn't believe me. Every angle of her face says so. "How?"

"I took a Lyft to her house," I spit out. "Do you wanna see the receipt?"

For a moment, it looks like she's about to say one thing. Then her expression flattens, and she raises her hand. "Know what? Never mind. Whatever."

"You should be happy for me!"

"Well, I'm not," Syd says. When she pushes off the wall, she rolls her eyes. "Pretend I didn't ask."

How dare she.

How. Dare. She.

All the arguments flow like lava, fire on the tip of my tongue. She's a liar too, she lied first, about the tattoo, she's lying about Hailey, she's lying to my *face*, and stealing all the moments from me that I surrendered willingly. But I don't say any of this; it moves too fast. I can't catch a single thought. Not a good one, anyway.

"Look, I'm sorry it didn't work out with Meghan—"

"This has nothing! To do! With Meghan!" Syd shouts.

Now people do look. A ripple passes through them; it wavers with anticipation. Fight, fight, fight. I shrink; Syd doesn't care about making a scene, but I do. I'm already *that* girl.

People have been waiting for *this* girl to crack for years. It's an idle hobby, bets unconsciously laid on the odds. Vegas spread: Will Ava lose it completely? Broken, traumatized, damaged people have to. That's what they think; it's the rules. It's even coverage. Nobody gets out alive—

(And here's the thing: they're not completely wrong. Finding out that one pinkie in the wrong place can send me back to the worst moment of my life—that's damage. Knowing I have to have a masturbation strategy in case my thoughts veer back to *that*—damage.)

(keeping a dead girl in the woods so no one will touch her)

(keeping a dead girl in the woods so no one will touch her, Ava)

I admitted it before—I'm broken—but I think everybody's broken in one way or another. Mine's written on my face and underneath my skin and deep in my brain, and things aren't always okay. But you know what?

Sometimes they are. Sometimes I'm fine. Maybe even most

times. So all these people peeping to see what's going to happen next in this prizefight, that's *their* brokenness.

They want bread and circuses and blood. They want glasses of wine thrown in somebody's face; they want to watch somebody stare into the camera and say *they are not here to make friends*—

Well, they're not getting that today.

Deliberate, I straighten up and clutch my bag. "Okay, then, when you're ready to quit lying to me about what it actually is, hit me up."

Something moves in me; it makes me glide. It keeps me off my knees; it lifts my head high. I walk away from my best friend, the best (mostly only) friend I've had all my life.

I don't look back, because I'm angry and you know what? I don't care what the world thinks. I don't care about the narrow gap that girls' feelings are supposed to fit in. I'm not sugar and spice and everything nice. I'm a human being—

I'm allowed to be angry.

IT'S HARD TO BE ANGRY AND ELATED AT TURNS. It all mashes into chaos, and I let moody take over. It's easier to be depressed about all the things that are wrong. It takes no effort at all, and Jane totally gets what I mean. Sitting on the edge of my desk in World Literature, she scuffs her nonexistent boots on the floor.

The room is dull and airless around her; one fluorescent bulb in the back ticks. It doesn't flicker. It just shifts from greenish light to greyish light, back and forth, unceasing. Jane swings her legs in time to it, listening to Mrs. Mendoza read dramatically from Ophelia's monologue in *Hamlet.*

Usually I like stuff like that, but today, it's getting on my nerves. Look at this beautiful lady who destroyed herself: Doesn't it make you feel bad for her boyfriend?

Our online book even has a gallery linked from the poem: a flood of wispy, watery women floating eyes wide open into death. It's supposed to be so beautiful, the way there's nothing left of her.

Jane twists to look back at me, her grin wry. "It's so cool the way girls die so dudes can have feelings."

Startled, I turn my FriXion marker over in my fingers. Until now, Jane has been whispers. Vague need. Now she's breaking down Shakespeare in the middle of Mendoza's class? I almost say something. Almost. Before the first sound gets out, I strangle it.

Nobody can hear her, but I'm pretty sure everybody can hear me. The school isn't so small that people are talking about the fight I had with Syd. But they would definitely talk about the girl with the scar chatting with invisible friends

(twenty-five bucks the basket case loses it by thanksgiving)

in English. Pulling the cap from my marker, I reply with long, lazy strokes along the edges of my color-coded, bullet-pointed notes. Ophelia. Psyche. Lot's Wife. Batman's mom. Every woman on *Supernatural* ever. Dead, dead, dead. The marker swishes easily in my hand as I unearth them.

Bad boys fall in love and reform just in time for their girlfriends to drop dead of cancer—beautiful, tragic cancer that never has puking or dementia or anything less aesthetic than a silvery tube of oxygen in a perfectly upturned nose. Or maybe she suddenly gets hit by a car when she's out for a bicycle ride in the rain. Or the pixie dust runs out of her manic dream state, and she commits glorious, meaningful suicide.

Fiction is greased with girlflesh and movies built on our bones: we are the reformers, the sanctifiers, the blood sacrifices. It's only sensible. That's how the world was built, too. Wars are waged on our backs, and no one talks about it. Nobody talks about the brothels in the concentration camps.

Comfort Women stay comfortably hidden outside our

textbooks. Joy Division is just a band name now. Historians gloss over rape in the pure white plantation houses, as if Sally Hemings ever had the opportunity to say no, as if her yes could mean yes when the man asking *owned* her.

Boudicca had to die, Anne Boleyn had to die, Ankhesenamun had to die, Marie Antoinette had to die.

Jane flicks her thumbnail with her forefinger. "I'm right there with them. The jolly rocks in some dude's spank bank. Just a memory. You think I'm a good one?"

My stomach roils, and a wet cotton weight fills my lungs.

I've always known, in my head, that he was out there somewhere. But even in the deepest folds and shadowiest synapses, I'd never, ever wondered if he thought about me. If he still *used* me. Not until now.

Dragging a hand over my mouth, I fall out of synch with the class. I don't hear Mendoza anymore. It's just me, just Jane. Just the scuff of her boot against cold linoleum. Just the cold weight of her skin next to the heat of mine. I have no idea who she really is; I haven't even tried to look.

I'm as bad as they are. And since we're supposed to have our iPads out, nobody notices when I slip out of our textbook app and into a search engine. *Missing teen maine*, I type, then click on *News* so I get everything recent. And recently, there are about 92,100 results. In .35 seconds, Google found 92,100 stories, and they're everywhere. Minot and Saco, Bangor and Harpswell.

As I scroll, their faces drift by. Some surprised, some open, some selfie perfect. The titles tell stories in quick reverse: Skowhegan woman still missing, Westbrook teen found safe, search continues for Gardiner girl. All of these people, gone, returned, lingering somewhere between.

My Jane isn't there. I think I'd recognize her, I really do. Even though her face is distorted beneath the tree and the snowpack, I smooth out her creases with my mind. I see her, after all, sitting right here with me. She reads over my shoulder avidly, humming under her breath. I can't make out the tune. It's familiar, but it won't name itself.

As the humming burrows into my brain, I try a new search: *Aquarius tattoo missing woman Maine*. I get nothing and garbage, but six or seven links down, I find the Wikipedia List of Unidentified Murder Victims in the United States. There's a *Wikipedia* page.

The bell grates on my nerves when it rings. I shoot from my chair and scoop all my stuff into my arms. No time to stop; no time to pack up. There's the slightest chance I'm freaking out. No, a pretty good chance, because I have a list of murder victims with no names, and I know there are websites full of missing people who are hopefully alive.

(funny funny funny I haven't tried that hard—at all—to find out who she is)

(oops, there goes a box flying open—)

I have Jane; I have her. Fine. I admit it. And I'm keeping her off both lists, for my own stupid, selfish reasons. Reasons I can justify less and less. Months and days and weeks have passed since I found her (just days, barely plural), and she's starting to fill up so much space, I breathe for two.

Jealousy or madness—tick a box: it has to be one of them. No, possessiveness; possession. Jealousy is different, but I can't weigh out the reasons why just now. An oily slick fug coats me as a thought, fully-formed, escapes.

What I'm doing is *wrong.*

I squirm into the hallway, through the door past a couple of my classmates. I don't know if I'm going to my next class or to the library or what. I'm just going, moving fast. Head down.

Turning up the main stairwell, I keep my shoulder to the wall and walk as fast as I can. I have a skeletal plan: locker, rearrange brain boxes, proceed. I never make it to the first step of the plan, though. When I hit the first floor landing, I see a face and I stop dead.

He's here.

The boy from the woods, from the Red Stripe. He's here.

I have found that my body also can keep silence.
—CASSIUS DIO, *ROMAN HISTORY*

But if there is any further injury,
then you shall appoint as a penalty life for life,
eye for eye, tooth for tooth, hand for hand, foot for foot,
burn for burn, wound for wound, bruise for bruise.
—EXODUS 21:23-25

1LOSTMARBLE STANDS IN FRONT OF ME, HANDS shoved in his battered jacket.

(i will find you)

Right there, in the open, in the full light—it's definitely him. He trembles like the skin of a drum, tight and ticking and dangerous. He doesn't belong here, and *no one* notices.

Guests are supposed to go through the office. The doors are supposed to be locked from the outside during the day. What if he had a gun? Wait, what if he *has* a gun?!

He senses me—lifting his head and staring into me. It doesn't matter that we're surrounded. His gaze cuts through the crowd—a hot knife, some thin ice. He shoves off the door and walks straight for me. People crash into him and bounce off his shoulders; he doesn't care. He doesn't stop.

If I run back, I'll be trapped in the basement. Run forward, and it'll be right into his arms. So I do the only thing my adrenaline lets me think of doing.

I swing my backpack hard to knock him off balance.

Girls' cries flutter to the ceiling like startled birds. My shoes squelch when I run past him. Protests fly up, because I'm not careful. I don't keep to the wall and keep my head down. Suddenly, I take up space when I never have before. Interesting, space, because running in the halls is a good way to get called out by a teacher.

Let them, let them, I figure because if I get hauled away, I get hauled away from him. He's behind me. I know he is; it's too loud to hear his footsteps, but I hear them. They fall hard. He reverberates—a stick that crashes against a cymbal.

I should run to Syd, I think. *No, I shouldn't. Things aren't okay. I should run to Hailey, but no, I shouldn't, because things would be ruined and I can't let them get that way.* To the Dean's office, to the parking lot, to the chem lab, with all its deadly possibilities.

Too much thinking. The Arts hallways swallow me up, and I'm past all the twists and turns I know well. Out of desperation, I fling myself at the double-tall, double-wide doors of the school auditorium. The left one holds. The right

(Things I Can!)

crashes open, and I stumble into the wings of the theater. Weights and ropes and pulleys stretch toward a distance ceiling. My boots clop on the old wooden floor. Velvet (maybe velvet—I don't know—thick! Thick!) curtains ripple when I shove past them, onto the stage. Only the aisle lights gleam in the dark, landing strips that lead back into darkness.

Halfway across, I realize I don't know what's on the other side. It could be cinder-block wall, all the way to the catwalk for all I know. This is not my place. I'm not safe here. I'm—

"S-ssstop!"

His voice is a high tenor hiss. He grabs me, and this time, I don't slip away. The force jerks me back. My bag and iPad and everything fly from my hands. Clattering across polished wood, the iPad turns on. The stage glows with manga fanart from *Hamilton*: A dot Burr with his pistol level, A dot Ham with his pointed at the air.

I've lived all the life I really remember in the After. Countless times, I've fantasized about what I'd do if it happened again. If someone came at me. I'm so practiced in daydreams.

Thumbs in eyes. Teeth through flesh. Banshee screams like daggers and tender bits mutilated. Always, always, *his* body hits the floor. I stand victorious, and no one ever touches me again.

And that's just not what happens.

Twisting, I struggle, and the sound that comes out of me is a warble. Snapping my teeth, I bite nothing but air. I think I'm saying, "Stop, stop," but maybe it's him. Tears sting my cheeks and clog my throat. It's going to happen here. Again. A hundred feet away from the Ceramics Studio. A hundred feet from safety.

"S-ssstop," he says. Definitely him; he wraps his arm around my shoulders. I'm pinned to him. Stretched on his chest, arched back like a martyr waiting for the arrows.

"I don't have your phone," I garble; I'm drowning on myself. "I gave it to the police."

He shifts behind me. His body moves against mine. I feel

him, too much of him, the angle of his hips and the heat from his skin and his arm pushing between us. Oh god, he's on me he's touching me he's—

This isn't supposed to happen again, plan or no plan, this *can't* be happening again! My heart is full of hate and fight, but I have no strength. Or maybe I have strength, but he's too strong. *(Stronger than me; stronger than Jane. She ended up dead in the woods. Where will he bury me?)*

He moves but not against me. There's silence, and then the theme song from *Doctor Who* starts to play. Tinny notes tinkle from inside my bag. His phone is ringing.

Haltingly he says, "It's not . . . what . . . you think."

I want to tell him he's proving that like a boss. Instead, I warble, and it's just a hopeless, helpless sound. Humiliating, useless.

The same door we crashed through swings open. Light spills across the stage. Salvation! My heart pounds so hard, I'm dizzy and my stomach lurches.

"I don't know what's going on in here," some unnamed teacher says, annoyed, "but if you make me come in there to find out, you're going to be sorry. Get to class!"

DO YOU REMEMBER WHEN I TOLD YOU ABOUT THE GUY who followed me home *after*? How he insisted on talking to my mom? How he told her what he saw, and the next thing I remember after that is Police-ER-Rape Kits-Superglue?

I hate him.

More than I hate the guy who raped me. The Good Samaritan, I wonder about *him.*

I wonder what he saw.

How long he watched.

Why he didn't call the police.

Why he didn't yell out the window, "Leave that girl alone!"

Whether he stopped to think about whether to follow me afterward and that's why he didn't show up until I'd already been home ten, fifteen minutes (crying and yelling at myself for crying and trying to hide the crying because I didn't want my mom to notice something was wrong—)

(Because I did wrong: I talked to a stranger. *I talked to a stranger,* and a terrible thing happened, and that made it *all my fault.*)

(Grade school logic. Not real logic. Just the logic of church and school and PSAs and guest speakers who happen to be police officers who are trying to help prevent One More Crime and those haters of girls previously mentioned: no matter how old or how young you are, no matter how bulletproof the story, there's always a way to blame the victim.

Why did you wear that dress? Why did you go to his room? Why did you let him buy you dinner? Why didn't you say no? Why didn't you say no *better*? Why were you out that late/on that side of town/drinking/toking/hitchhiking/smoking/hooking up with somebody you met online? Why did you talk to the stranger?

WHY DID YOU TEMPT THE BAD MAN?)

—and he showed up at the back gate and insisted. He made me get my mom. He wouldn't go away. He didn't take no for an answer, and yeah, probably he *shouldn't* have, but there were other things he shouldn't have done, either. Like watching. Like waiting. Like closing the barn door after the horses.

I hate that man.

And I hate the teacher at the door, because she doesn't wait. She doesn't frog-march us, me and Jane's murderer, out of the theater. No questions, no realization that I'm a legitimate student at Aroostook and *he's* a homicidal outsider trying to take me out under their roof. No write-ups, no detention slips. Just a vague threat and vanishment.

The only good to come out of this moment is that 1LostMarble lets me go. Abruptly. And I end up stumbling away from him. Freedom still feels like a trap. I wrap my arms around my bag and spin toward him. To attack, to scream, to—

He's looking at his freaking phone and texting somebody!

Except, then a mechanical voice scrabbles up between us. A program, like the one on his *other* phone, the one in my bag, says for him, "I need it. It has all my evidence."

Revulsion crawls up the inside of my rib cage. "You mean your souvenirs?"

Another long pause as he types; he holds up his mobile again. "I didn't hurt her," it says. His face, frustrated and insistent, agrees, "She was my friend."

I take a step back. "Not mutually exclusive."

"I know who did."

I can't, can't, can't believe I'm standing in semidarkness with a killer, listening to him talk with a text-to-speech thingie on his phone. Like, he should be wearing half a mask and a cloak and rise up in the smoke behind me or something. It's creepy and wrong, and *Great, why don't you keep on talking to him, Ava?* "Then why didn't you go to the cops already?"

Frustration flashes up in his dark eyes. He shakes his head; it echoes all down his body. He's annoyed and frustrated, and he points at my bag. He doesn't have to speak; I understand. Whatever he has that will convince me, I've already got in my possession.

I don't know the right thing to do. My knees wobble, encouraging me to sink to the floor and cry. That fixes up this little red wagon, doesn't it? Crying? Very helpful. Clutching the bag tighter, I say nothing.

He types at me furiously. "Pics of license plates! Chat

screenshots! Cleared the whole phone except for stuff about this. Evidence!"

Wavering, I search his face. There has to be some sign he's lying. Or a light that will tell me he's not. I want to find it. I want to know for sure, but all there is is a face. Dark brows, brown eyes, high cheekbones, thin lips. Some color slapped into his cheeks, some hair falling across his forehead. He looks ordinary.

(Most people do.)

"You don't need evidence to talk to somebody," I say, uncertain. I know why *I* kept Jane; my reason is good. My reason is reasonable.

"Cop's nephew did it," he replies. Then he arches a brow and points at my bag again.

Suddenly, it's all there in my head. The gallery I was so afraid to open, the one that didn't have an archive of Jane's body, but instead, cars. License plates. The cruiser in the driveway in the snow. The unnerving lack of texts and mails and chats. The only signs of life some screenshots from Discord—pieces of conversations that made no sense out of context.

Context. I start to crack at the edges. He might be telling the truth. And when sheer panic drops away, I tremble. All that adrenaline has to go somewhere. It pools in my hands and feet, leaving me shaky and numb.

"How'd you find her?" I ask.

"Tracked her phone till it disappeared. Searched." He lifts his chin in defiance. "You?"

"IT WAS AN ACCIDENT."

That's what I say, but I don't believe that.

I was supposed to find her. I was supposed to keep her safe. I am her keeper and her guardian; I'm her sister and her best friend. Jane and I walk in the same skin. I breathe for her.

"You don't know her. I do. Just let me have it."

Relief hangs just out of reach. That would be easy: surrender everything to him and let whatever happens happen. Let Jane go before I have to admit what I've done. Before I have to really think about why I did it. Boxes upon boxes tumbling open in my mind. Everything spilling out, everything mixing together.

With a knot in my throat, I say, "You could be lying about all of this."

He shrugs. The expression says it all. Yeah, he could. He could be the second coming of Ted Bundy, for all I know. But he could just as easily be King Arthur in black.

Thumbs sliding on his phone, he stares at the screen, then looks up at me as he hits Enter. "I didn't attack you." The voice on the phone doesn't have emphasis, but he flashes his eyes at me on *you*.

History isn't always what happened; it's how the people who lived it remember it. We study the Revolutionary War, and we call it American. George Washington seems *American*, but he wasn't at first. Alexander Hamilton wasn't American, Thomas Jefferson, Benjamin Franklin, not American—they were *British*.

The British weren't coming; the British were already here. Those forefathers were *traitors* right up until the moment they won the war.

And so, I see 1LostMarble's point. I don't like it, but I see it. Let's say he's telling the truth—and I think maybe, possibly, he *is*—who am I in this situation?

I'm the stranger who appeared in the night while he stood over a friend's clandestine grave. I'm the stalker who lingered in his store for hours watching him work. I'm the thief; I might even be the pervert. This war isn't over yet; we don't know who wins. I tell this story, but I could be the villain. The villain never thinks they're wrong. *Oh god, am I wrong?*

"I need to think about this," I say. "I can't do this here."

He looks like he might throw his phone on the ground. He makes a move, like he's going to approach me, but then he stops. Rasping frustrated fingers through his hair, he thumbs in a one-word response. "Why?"

"It's complicated."

When he speaks aloud, I fully realize why he's using an electronic voice. He's angry, and his words don't fall out fluently. The consonants repeat; the vowels drag. He has a stutter, one that trips over itself when he shouts, "You-you're c-c-razy! Just . . . give it to me!"

The stage floor creaks as I move toward the door. "Meet me after school."

"Where?"

Good question. I say the first thing that comes to mind. "Wescott's Coffee, downtown."

He's reluctant. Still annoyed. He thinks he's negotiating with a terrorist, but that's too bad. I have leverage, and I have questions. I'm not letting him decide Jane's fate alone. I'm just not. So he can meet me or give up on getting his evidence/phone back.

I skirt around him. My footsteps echo in the auditorium. The second bell is about to ring

(or maybe it did and I missed it?)

and I'm going, no matter what. It's not that I care about being late to class (okay, I care a little). But I need to get away, take a breath. Get my thoughts together.

The last few days have been chaos. Elation and drugged; all my unhoped-for wishes coming true and all my worst fears rising up in a snow-covered grave. Pushed by Syd, pulled by Hailey—I can't think clearly. And that's what I need right now. Clarity.

Backing toward the door, I ask, "Are you going to be there? We get out at two fifty."

His jaw is tight and there's an irritated vein flickering in his throat. But he nods, and now I have a date with a killer. Or with an ally. Jane's friend. Someone who actually knows her. Someone who knows her name.

And I am selfish. I don't ask it. For a little while longer, she remains my Jane.

There is heat.

There's heat in the ground, and it rises.

Slowly, because the earth is all about slow. Tectonic-plate-motion slow. Geologic-time slow. All that lethargy is essential. If the ground shifted like the sun, nothing would grow. The earth takes seasons to shift—early snow is early snow.

It isn't ice.

It isn't permafrost.

It isn't permanent.

That prehistoric Ice Man in the Alps had tundra and eternal winter to tide him over until that glacier encased him in ice. Those mummies in the Andes have cold air and stone to keep them, until everything in them turns to leather.

Northern Maine has no tundra, no permafrost, no glaciers lurking. It has snow that comes early, but earth that still warms. And worms. Things alive in it still live; things dead on it are still dead. And while the large predators find the small delicacies, the small predators wait for just enough heat, just a little warmth, to start their feast.

Inside out because bacteria don't need to breathe—but they have breath.

That breath makes marks on skin, it mottles flesh, it exhales gases. It's hot air from the inside: puffing up everything soft, pushing out everything that's soft. Tongues and eyes and other organs near other holes . . .

All those archaeologists who find remains and say, "It looks like she just fell asleep yesterday!" are lying.

They lie because no body—not Ötzi the Iceman or the Andes Ice Maiden or the climbers who failed to climb down from Mount Everest—looks as if they fell asleep yesterday. That lie makes us feel better. It makes us believe in all the bodies on television that are nothing more than blue lipstick and grey powder.

You know it's a lie because you've been to a funeral. You've heard someone say, "Look how peaceful . . ." and maybe even, "Just like they're sleeping." You know in your heart, your still-beating heart, that it's a lie. But you take the lie, you chew the lie, you swallow the lie.

If you didn't, you might never stop screaming,

The dead, even the recently deceased and gently preserved, primped and powdered and wearing clothes someone else picked out for them—they do not look like they're peaceful or asleep.

And neither does she. Especially because the earth is warm, and it radiates, slowly, upward, inexorable.

The worms don't crawl in. They don't crawl out.

But bodies are full of living things. What they do from the inside is so much worse than what a few well-meaning worms might do looking for a place to weather the storm—

Well, it's really better if you don't think about it. Just enjoy the nursery rhyme instead.

I TEXT MY MOTHER FROM A BATHROOM STALL. Going to be late tonight; hanging out w/ Hailey. A truth—not all of it.

I'm not sure I like you going out so much on school nights.

My head jerks back. Did not expect that. I really didn't. She was mad when I was blowing in late or when I was out without telling her—those made sense.

And when she told me I needed to let her know if I was going to be late, that order stuck. But now she just randomly doesn't want me going out on a school night? Like she knows anything about what I do? I compose a couple of replies, deleting and rewriting until I have one that doesn't sound annoyed. I'll make sure I'm back before eleven.

Invite her over, Mom says. Order pizza. Double pepperoni, on me.

No. That's not what I want. We're supposed to go flying: music on the radio, darkness outside, black threads of highway unfurling as we drive everywhere, nowhere. Maybe we'd go to the fire tower again. Stand like queens together above our strange, silent nation. Sitting in my house, with pizza, how am I supposed to brush the wild, flyaway strands of Hailey's hair from her face?

Not gonna happen. She keeps kosher.

Mom's response is almost instant. Veggie lovers, then.

Please? We already have plans.

What plans?

Jeez, Mom, come on! I rack my brain, and I can't think of a way to honestly say what we're doing without telling her that we're just going driving. Because I don't think she'd like it.

I can come up with the reasons why all on my own: the weather, the roads (mostly okay now), the darkness, the youth of the driver, the make of the car, something.

So my reply is imprecise. We're just hanging out. Watching movies.

Her answer: Netflix and chill?

Rolling my eyes so hard, I stand up and lean against the wall. Leave it to my mother to not only dredge up ancient slang but to deploy it accurately. My face gets hot with a blush, because I'm nowhere near ready for "and chill," and also, my mom literally just asked me if I'm having sex with someone in the most antique way possible.

I touch the microphone icon and say, "No comma mother period. Netflix and homework period."

Fine. Go tonight. Tomorrow night, we're going to have a talk.

Oh, good. A talk.

Gathering up my stuff, I glower, complaining in my own head. She's never done this to me. We don't fight. We really don't; most of the time she's great. Treats me like an adult, trusts me to do the right thing.

The water comes out ice-cold; I shiver as I scrub my hands in it. I guess all that trust came easy, since I didn't go anywhere or do anything. Approved outings with her; sanctioned time with Syd, who calls her Mom, too. Tension snakes around me, thinning my breath. She wants to keep Rapunzel in the Tower; she's decided I need a trim.

Realizing I don't want one feels like a bubble popping and light pouring out. I lean over the sink and face myself in the mirror. Me, my scar . . . and behind me, Jane. She's amused, shaking her head at me.

"What's so funny?" I ask her.

Jane holds up a hand, her fingertips missing. All of her fingertips are missing, little shards of bone sticking up just past her flesh.

Mom doesn't want to fight. She never wanted to fight. She just had to and lost, and now I'm giving her a hard time. I plunge my hands under the icy water again. It's a shock the second time. When I splash my face, I gasp.

It's like a slap, and I come to.

I'm talking to a dead girl. Meeting with a stranger who could still be her killer. Hiding a dead body in the tree line above the Aroostook River. And I'm fighting with my mom about leaving the house. About my *curfew.* This is so messed up.

I am so very, very messed up.

I AM NOTHING BUT ALL CAPS. I'M TWITCHY AND TOO full; there's too much in my skin. Every time someone closes a door, I jump. The hallway between classes was a roar that never ended.

And now, the sound of fingers on keyboards in the library is constant thunder. I *should* be in Econ. I *should* be parsing out $A=P(1+r)^Y$ against the average cost of five different secondary education options, i.e., how much the compound interest is if I go to Harvard instead of Northern Maine Community College.

But I skipped Econ because the answer is A L O T and W H O C A R E S ? because I just had a conversation with a guy who threatened to find me, managed to find me, and claims he didn't kill Jane, even though I caught him standing over her body *twice.* Do I have a coffee date with Jeffrey Dahmer?

My life was good and fine and *tethered.* All the boxes were sorted and sealed and stacked. A place for everything; everything in its place. Me at Syd's side with nobody else, really. Me at home every night immediately after school. Me at home, gorging on Korrasami fanfic with a heaping side of Stucky. Me with other people's hopes and dreams and philosophies needled into my skin. It was a good house. It was a good life.

And then, her.

Before Jane, I barely thought about *him*. I sometimes felt him. But only sometimes. I had my scar, but it wasn't open; it didn't bleed. It didn't bloom and beat with my heart and threaten to split me in half. I wasn't

(a basket case)

ripped up, tripped up, cutting class, driving without a license, lying and lying and lying—

I was *safe*

(but I wasn't falling in love)

(touching lips, touching palms)

(flying in the night).

I keep dragging my hands into my hair and twisting. Hard. I can't tell if I'm trying to keep from crying or trying to make myself sob. People don't look over; the library, at least, is a bastion of people who want to be alone—who long for a place to be still, to be quiet, to escape.

That's why we all look up when Syd sweeps in. She has keys and tiny bells and other dangly, jangly things sewn to her jacket. Each step is a song, a merry whisper, and seeing her come toward me is like a light. A brightness right in the middle of my chest, the possibility of . . .

What?

Salvation? Hope? A whole new escape, I don't know. It just feels good to see her walk toward me. Like, I want to jump up and hug her and hide in all her familiarity. I turn in my chair; my chair doesn't turn with me. It traps me in the carrel so I half rise, then fall back down when Syd arrives.

"So are you still on the rag or what?"

.

.

.

I don't realize I'm yelling in the library until it's already happening. A torrent of fury spills out, magma rolling inexorably through my words. I couldn't stop them if I tried. I don't even want to.

"Are you done being a jealous bitch?"

Syd rears back. Her brows fly sky high, ash-blond against the blue of her curls. "Oh, you did not."

"Oh yes I did," I say. "Because that's what this is about, right?"

"I don't even know what 'this' is, Ava!"

I bend my fingers back so fast counting that they hurt. "Your attitude, your mean-girl texts, your kidding-not kidding—"

"How about your"—she mirrors me, mocks me, counting with her fingers—"attitude and lies and screw-Syd-I've-got-a-girlfriend bull—"

"Ladies!" barks the librarian. She shoves herself to her feet and starts toward us. This isn't a silent library, but it's quiet. Usually, people don't scream in each other's faces.

I try to push my chair back again. It tips from under me. I grab the edge of the carrel; somehow I stay on my feet as the chair crashes to the carpet. "I don't have an attitude, and the rest of it is— Wow, I don't even know!"

With a quick glance back, Syd judges how far the librarian is from us, and how much she can get away saying before she arrives. There's probably a physics equation for this, but we're just estimating. Turning back to me, Syd says, "You don't even know because you don't *want* to know."

"I don't know because you don't tell me—"

"Ladies!" the librarian yells. She steps between us. Her voice is firm and icy; she doesn't have to lay a hand on us to move us. "To the office. Now."

THE LIST OF THINGS I'VE NEVER DONE IS GETTING shorter and shorter.

> ~~*Never snuck out.*~~
> ~~*Never drove a car alone.*~~
> ~~*Never cut class.*~~
> ~~*Never got detention.*~~
> ~~*Never held hands.*~~
> ~~*Never been kissed.*~~
> *Never had sex (?technically? girlginity intact, boyginity uh . . . ?)*
> ~~*Never climbed a fire tower.*~~
> ~~*Never stalked someone.*~~
> ~~*Never hid a body in the woods.*~~

I have detention for a week. My mother. Is going. To kill me.

But hey, I'm having *new experiences*! The only things I can do are smile in disbelief and marvel at myself while I sit in room 415, by the radiator, amazed that detention just looks like bored kids doing homework.

Wow. Just wow.

I did manage to shoot off a text to Hailey; I didn't tell her I had detention. I said I had to stay after to talk to a teacher. This is half a lie and barely counts as I *am* staying after. And I *did* talk to Mr. Monogan.

I'd said, "Do I sign in here?"

And he'd said, "Yep. Take a seat wherever."

So now that I think about it, I didn't lie at all. And lying to myself about how I'm *not* lying to Hailey makes me hate myself a little.

God, I am such a mess. When she finds out, she's going to run as fast as she can, far, far away from me and all my disaster. And she should. She really should.

Rubbing my eyes, I dip my head just long enough for Mr. Monogan to say, bored, "No sleeping."

Now my face flames, and tears spring up. Out of reflex, I glance to the other side of the room, where Syd set up camp after she arrived. She stares at Canvas on her iPad, probably uploading homework or digging around for the link to one textbook or another.

Even here, she looks comfortable. Collected. Her curls spill over her shoulders; her matte lips purse thoughtfully. I wonder what it's like for everything to be fine. What it's like to have a life where nothing really, truly awful ever happened. That's probably not fair,

(she has problems; she cries; she hurts)

but right now, I just don't care. It's her fault we're in detention.

She lied to me first. She's *still* lying to me. And now she's just . . . sitting over there, *fine.* My guts churn and my face burns and I could laugh or cry hysterically at any moment, and she's *fine.*

I suck in a sharp breath and cut my gaze toward the window. Jane lounges there in the reflection, comfortable in her plaids and her jeans. She drums the exposed bones of her fingertips on the desk, *dra-dada-dum*, again and again until it almost becomes a melody.

Maybe I've misunderstood since the beginning. Maybe Jane is real, and I'm not. Maybe I'm the body in the woods, stripped of everything, even breath. It could be, it could actually be, that I've been dead this whole time, one *Sixth Sense* away from cliché: not seeing dead people; being them.

Letting go, I lose myself in Jane's lazy rhythm. I stare at nothing; I bother no one. This is all right. I am quietly nothing. I barely exist.

I am not real.

HAILEY LEAVES ME WITH A KISS OUTSIDE WESCOTT'S Coffee.

She's going to strength training, and she thinks I'm going to do my homework and wait for her. This after she already swung back around to school to pick me up after I "talked to" Mr. Monogan. It hits me again: we're barely together and I'm lying to her.

And I'm using her, because I needed a ride. I let her waste her time for me because I needed a ride.

My birthday and Christmas money is running out. If Mom looks at my bank account, she's going to see a charge for Lyft, and I can't explain it. Can't ask Syd, obviously. Can't drive myself: still no license, no idea when I'm gonna get one.

I don't want to be this person, and at the exact same time, I don't know how *not* to be this person. Mr. Burkhart is obsessed with pinpointing the moment the American experiment really began in history. I'm positive that in the Ava experiment, the moment I became Ava-After, began when that man ran his finger down my face. He drew the map in my flesh, and it inexorably led here.

(*Lies, lies, lies*, my head sings.)

It's the path I'm on. So I push into the warmth of the coffee shop. The air is bittersweet, heavy with coffee and bright with cinnamon. Music jangles low in the background, something acoustic and plinky. For a moment, time twists and it's two months into the future. The cold behind me; the heat before me. It feels like Christmas.

It feels like everything is okay.

Then 1LostMarble drops a hand on my shoulder. He drags me back to October with two words typed into his phone. "Over here."

There are already two cups on the table. Nice but also evidence that I'm really late. As I sink into the chair across from him, I peel off my gloves, but I don't reach for the cup.

That's one of the cardinal rules, ladies. Watch your glass, never leave it unattended, don't take a drink if you didn't see the bartender/barista make it. (Has anybody ever said, "Hey, gentlemen, don't put drugs in people's drinks?" Have those words ever been lined up in that order, in history, ever?)

"So?" he asks, typing two letters into his phone to produce the question.

And so help me god, the impulse to ask him what happened crashes into me like a train. I mean, I heard the stutter, so that's probably why. But still my brain picks at it. Has he always been this way? Is he in therapy? Why is he using a phone instead of . . . I don't know, an official talking box. It's all rude and none of my business, and I have to fight myself not to ask.

(Not to be the same as all those people who look at me and wonder.)

The reason I win the fight is because I hate the answering. I hate that the question exists at all—people are people and variegated, and *that's what happened.* I have a scar; he uses his phone to talk. Nature, nurture, evolution, epigenetics, something that feels good in the summer: that's what happened.

"Hello?"

He waves a hand in front of me, to snap me out of it. Out of reflex, I reach for the cup in front of me. I will not drink. *I won't,* I warn myself. But I do wrap my cold fingers around the steamy cardboard.

"Start from the beginning," I say.

Annoyance sparks across his face. Pressing his lips together, he types angrily and then glowers when the phone delivers his reply in monotone. "How about you start at the beginning?"

Fine. I gather a breath. I summarize my week. One paragraph. Simple.

"The day of the big snow, I was walking home, following the river. I started up the hill to get to the road. I slipped and knocked a log over, and there she was. I covered her back up, and I left. Now you."

With an incredulous laugh, he stares at me a moment, then says, "That's not all. You came back."

"To check on her!"

"You didn't call the police."

"Because I didn't . . ." I stop. My mouth goes dry as old leather.

The reason why is simple and complicated. It's logical and

(basket case)

reasonless. Sucking my tongue to wet my mouth again, I squeeze the cup of coffee, little strokes of pressure that make the lid pop up, then collapse. Finally, I choose accuracy without precision. "I was afraid."

This time, he snorts at me. "Of what?"

"The police," I say sharply. Something in his expression softens, and I go on. "And when I saw you there, I thought you did it. I assumed you did it. I was trying to catch *you*."

"You attacked me."

"I was protecting her," I say.

"Decked me with a flashlight."

Rigid, I say, "Fine." I don't want to call it that, but fine. We can brush past that and get to the point. "I attacked you. And we both know what's happened since then. So now your turn. Start from the beginning. How did you find me?"

"The same way I found her."

After the voice stops, he swipes across his phone and adjusts something on the screen. Then he slides it in front of me. Anticipating the question, he already wrote out a wall of text to answer it. Is that smart and logical, or is that terrifying? I can't decide.

The first line starts, *I met Lark—*

A little earthquake runs beneath me; a stiletto slips between my ribs. I look up, catching a glimpse of Jane just as she dissolves. My friend, my sister—the one who haunted me and shared my skin—unbecomes. No more denim jacket, no more heavy boots.

No more knowing looks, amused or annoyed or leading.

Now there is Lark. A stranger with the same face, someone new. Someone I've never met.

Trembling, I look back at the screen.

I met Lark playing Rust. She broke into my base like a boss, but she didn't gank me or steal my stuff. She put up signs on all the walls. Painted them with stars and moons. Wrote stuff like, *Anarchy Interior Design* and *This Base Improved by ArcanePriestess.* That's her handle in the game.

We talked all the time on Discord, we were **friends.** She was fighting a lot with her mom. Her mom kept kicking her out. She'd couch surf for a while, then the cops would show up to bring her home because her mom reported her missing. It got really bad at home, and Lark started talking about getting emancipated or whatever.

The next thing I know, she's hitchhiking from Provo across the country. I'm keeping track of her on Google Maps, just in case. She says she's going to visit everybody she knows from online. People from Rust, people from Minecraft, I think somebody from Overwatch.

She's, like, there are two of you in Maine. I'll visit him, then I'll visit you. I told her she could crash with me as long as she needed to.

> The whole trip, she texted me, pix, etc., but the night she was supposed to meet this other guy, nothing. I was worried. Her phone was in Walker's Corner, but it wasn't moving. So I found the other guy on Discord and asked what was up. He said he never saw her. When I pinged him again, he ignored me.
>
> Her phone was still live, so I went to it. Her phone and her bag, I found in a dumpster in Walker's Corner. I found her jeans in the woods. Then I found her.

As I read, I purse my lips. It sounds real, but I'm not the best judge of character, am I? Returning his phone, I ask, "Did she know you were stalking her?"

He frowns. His thumbs fly. "I wasn't stalking her. I was keeping an eye on her."

An answer that doesn't instill all the confidence in the world. And I sit there a moment, and realize what he said, in the beginning. *The same way I found her.* My throat closes, but I manage to ask, "So you hacked into my email account?"

He shrugs. "You took something from me. I needed it back."

"Show me," I say. I don't want to be closer to him, but I pull my chair closer. I want to see this dark magic on his phone; I want to see the rabbit and the hat at the same time. "Show me how you found me."

This time, he speaks aloud, carefully. "It's not h-h-hard."

And then he shows me just how easy it is. He already had one email address for me: school. That gave him my real name from the online yearbook. My real name gave him my gmail address, and a little app on his phone hashed through the password. With the password, he logged into my account and

Oh

My

God

It's just right there. Google Location. Timeline. Bright red dots showing every place I've been for the last couple of years. My trips to Mount Desert to see my dad. My failed week at Hirundo.

Zoom in, and there's Syd's house, over and over. There's Hailey's house. The school. What I assume is the fire tower, because that dot is in the middle of nowhere.

Switching to his speech app, he asks, "You wanna see all your Google searches? You spend an awful lot of time trying to find out how to get special cats to come to your Neko game. Also? You searched for missing girls with an Aquarius tattoo."

I want to throw up on the table. In his lap. I want to cover my head and wrap myself in a billion blankets. All this time, I thought I was safe in my house. Safe and hidden and *safe* and . . .

I excuse myself to get a cup of water. I need cold to pour down my throat, to ice me from the inside. I need to repack my boxes. I need to run.

BUT I DON'T, BECAUSE WHEN I LOOK IN THE MIRROR, Jane—*Lark*—is still there. She reflects me as I drink from the tap and scrub my wrist across my mouth to dry it. Her hands funnel into her hair as mine do the same. She is me; I am her.

"What am I supposed to do?" I ask her.

Her lips move only so long as mine do. She blinks when I blink. When I exhale and look away, she does the same.

A splinter of a thought lodges in my mind: What if I haven't seen her at all? Not in my room, not in bed. Not in front of Mom's car, not in mirrors or glass or curves of polished metal. Not in class, not at home. Not at all.

What if I imagined . . .

(that is not a thought i can have)

(I have to get a box, a new box, stuff that thought down,

down,

down,

compress it until it's nothing but a seed. Fit it in the tiniest box; that's right. Wrap it with duct tape and tie it up tight. We're not going there again. We're never going there again.)

But I am going back to the table, where 1LostMarble sits. It's funny how no one around us notices anything. Wearing bright beanies, stuffed into overstuffed coats, people come and go at Wescott's Coffee, and they never seem to cast a look at me or 1LostMarble, not even once.

We look like two kids, one chai, one mocha—we could almost be cute. This could be my adorable coffee shop meet-cute, ha: he lost his phone, I found his phone, what comes next is charming misunderstanding, inexplicable attraction, and a sweet, foamy finale where we fall in love.

My head spins. No one cares. It's almost funny how hard I work to seem okay; it's almost funny how little it seems to matter.

Tapping into his phone, 1LostMarble hits Send and the bored, robotic voice says, "So can I have it back or what?"

A tale of two cell phones. I take his and I type but don't hit Send: "Why didn't you go to the police?"

1LostMarble spreads his hands out, exasperated. Then he rolls his eyes and takes the phone to reply in text. "I'm on probation."

When I rear back, he rolls his eyes again. Typing faster now, he turns the screen to me, typos and all. I read right over them; on the list of important things right now, perfect presentation is way down at the bottom.

> You know those digital signs over the highway? The ones that tell you if there's road construction coming up? I hacked into a bunch of them for a prank.

I don't understand, and I say so with a frown. He types again, for a long time, then shoves the phone under my nose again.

> I reprogrammed them to say stuff like "The Cake is a Lie" and "Zombies Ahead, Run!!" It was a joke, but the state doesn't have a sense of humor. They tracked me down and arrested me for destroying public property. I didn't destroy dick but w/e.
>
> Cops dragged me out of work in handcuffs. Took away my phone, so when they questioned me, I couldn't answer. The stutter gets worse when I'm nervous. Everything just shuts down, right? But they thought I was screwing around.
>
> I was in there for hours until my dad showed up. Got a plea bargain: no jail but probation. Not supposed to use computers, etc. So I knew everything had to be correct and tight before I went to the cops. Then I find out the guy who did it lives with a cop.
>
> So.

So.

Under the whir of the coffee grinder, I fold my hands together. Lace my fingers up, squeezing so hard my knuckles ache. I feel the rumble of the inevitable. It's a choice: right or left; *Things I Can, Things I Can't.*

This cold snap won't last forever. I can't save Jane. Like, literally, I can't keep her much longer. Even if rotting waits for spring, well. I've seen her hands, her fingers, with the tips bitten off. She's delicious, and wild beasts and creatures can't be blamed for their hunger.

Keeping her will destroy her, and without this dude's evidence, Jane gets touched and violated for nothing.

I know absolute squat about her. But he—

He has those game chats and background information, and god, he knows where her clothes and her phone are, too. Locked inside him: her name, her hometown, the last fight she had with her mom. The people she knows; the ones she meant to get to know.

Who really hurt her. Where that monster lives.

A headache splits my brain in two. Funny how neither of us went to the authorities. The police I don't trust because I know what they would do to solve her; the police he doesn't trust because this guy is related to one of their own *and* he's afraid he'll end up in jail. Here we are, balanced on either side of a scale.

The two of us, we're not friends. We're not even acquaintances. We're two perpendicular paths. We crossed; we won't cross again. Our intersection is bright. It burns.

In the distance, there is the rumble of the inevitable. I'm not the only one who knows where she is; she will be exposed. The ice won't keep forever. Winter can't stop time, only slow it. And if he gives her up, the cops might never look past *him* to get to *her*.

We have to do this my way. Whatever evidence is left, we collect it. We make the case airtight: no questions, no doubt. Then I'll deliver it in a white-girl-perfect-victim package. 1LostMarble never even talks to the cops. I pretend I'm Girl Sherlock, and I dazzle them with everything they need.

Fait accompli.

So, I don't reach for my bag. I don't give him the phone he came for. Instead, I ask, "What do we still need?"

And then, almost as an afterthought, I add, "And what is your name?"

ON STEADY FEET, I WALK OUT OF THE COFFEE SHOP.

The cold outside is an assault, but I don't care. His name is Nick. He's going to call me. He's not happy about any of this, but he doesn't get a say.

My whole body aches. It's like somebody beat me up. (I may be that somebody.) There's that buzz in my head again. The too-much buzz, the weight of emotions as they snap and break free. Boxes tumble open, and my thoughts are a screaming, jumbled mess. I'm being pulled into pieces, and I know what I want.

I want to run down the alley, the one that goes to the river. I want to throw myself at Amber and tell her to tattoo whatever she wants. Just give me a new skin to be in. Make me over; transform me into an unknown Ava, a brand-new Ava. One whose body *he* would never recognize.

One that's better and fearless, and knows what to say when her best friend goes haywire. One that holds hands any which way—just dig the needle in deep and draw a new map of me, one so bright and vivid and fierce that no one sees the scar anymore.

But I don't. I don't have the money. I don't have the time.

I want to be brave enough to give up my flesh, but I'm not. I'm not, I'm not; and I duck into the candle shop and ask to use the bathroom.

There's too much perfume in the air. Warm wax that smells like "seaside" and "pumpkin patch" and "vanilla dreams" competes with musk and ancient spices and patchouli. It's a nightmare herb garden, and I want to vomit.

The bathroom door is warped. It takes two hard shoulder-checks to get it to close all the way.

Here it smells like bleach and some vague, blue antiseptic. I press a hand against the wall above the toilet.

Just do it, I tell my stomach. In reply, my stomach roils but retracts. Shrinking to a hard stone in my belly, it becomes a weight. My body doesn't obey, and I wonder, does anyone's?

Why can't it just turn itself inside out? If I could scrape the insides clean, put myself back together, maybe it would be all right.

Instead, I hover over a chipped toilet, trying to make my throat sour. Wishing for that tang to goad my guts, but nothing. Instead, I stand there, hot face, cold skin, and just feel sick.

All at once, my throat tightens and my nose stuffs up. I cry, suddenly and ug-ily. A teenage tragedy mask.

My lips twist; a quiver ripples through my chin. Each sob drags a hook through my chest. It catches under my breastbone and yanks, again and again.

I am so screwed up.

Maybe too screwed up.

Too broken for friends, too broken to fall in love, too broken to live in this stupid, screwed-up world. I want to sit and sob, but I'm not so broken that I'm willing to put my butt on a public bathroom floor. It's stupid how things like that persist. How reality seeps into emotionality.

Sure, yes, definitely, have a nervous breakdown, but ugh, don't do it on community tile.

That thought thins the tears. I shove off the wall. Dropping my bag onto my feet, I drape my coat over my arm so neither one touches the dirty floor and then I turn on the sink. The water runs clear and cold. Scooping a handful to my mouth, I drink and wash away the taste of nothing. I cut through the slime just under my nose; I scrub off the tears and erase their tracks.

This, I tell myself, *is over.*

This lunatic fugue state ends here. Wash up. Straighten up. Meet Hailey at the gym. Watch her defy physics with her lean, strong body, then hold her hand over the console in her car.

Go home by ten. Have that talk with Mom. Fix it up. Tie it all up with a ribbon. Yes. And hey, maybe I'll even reach out to Syd. Not to say sorry, because this time she has to apologize. But just to see—

And no more Jane, because there *is* no more Jane. Same for 1LostMarble, because he's Nick now. Nick, who's going to help me take care of his friend. All is well, and all is as it should be.

And why do I believe him? I believe him, I think, because I have to. It puts an axis through the middle of the globe. It keeps me from spinning even more wildly out of orbit. It's reasonable, rational

(I'm desperate)

and that's how this ends. We'll take care of Jane, and then I'll walk back into my life like I never stepped out of it. I'll rearrange the boxes more carefully. He'll go in one; Jane goes in another—

Not Jane.

Lark.

The *L* sits on the tip of my tongue, a little acid, a little bitter. The steady beat of my brains against my skull makes it hard to concentrate. It also makes it easy to say nothing out loud. Just like I let her body hide in the woods, I can let her name hide in my heart.

Until I speak it. Until I give her up.

But not yet.

Once upon a time, there was an Egyptian pharaoh named Hatshepsut, who shared the crown with her seriously ticked-off half brother Thutmose. He wanted to be all the pharaoh, but she was older, wiser, people liked her—

And when she died before him, he sent people out across all of Egypt to chip her legacy off every single wall and statue and column they could find, leaving sandstone wraiths where once had been her name.

If no one remembers you, *they thought,* then you are annihilated.

But that's thousands of years ago (and obviously, Thutmose missed a couple of inscriptions).

The girl in the woods—there are people who know her name. She's only been dead a few days, and she had lots of friends. Online and off, all around—she's dead, but she'll live on a little longer. She left early; people remain. They don't even realize they know her in the past tense, yet.

Some of them remember her third-grade picture, with giant front teeth and slightly crossed eyes. Maybe some of them remember the Rose Tico costume she wore to Halloween last year. Some know her by her digital traces; some, by her flesh.

But the flesh is faltering. Snow melting. Earth warming. Worms worming.

And the truth . . . the truth is everyone is dead for much longer than they're alive. So the people who remember her name now might go on, for decades, whole collections of them.

But one by one, they'll go dark—stars in the night sky, dying. One by one, the people who can say they knew her will sink into earth themselves. One day, they'll be forgotten too.

It's almost like our natural state is death.

Life is a deviation, the briefest of intermissions, before we return to the dark.

"IS EVERYTHING OKAY?" HAILEY ASKS AS SHE PULLS into the gas station.

The Admiral is closed at this hour, and it's the last stop before we hit the Canadian border.

It's an old service station. The pumps don't have digital numbers on them, just black and white dials—the kind that slowly spin to the correct amount. Orangey overhead lights dirty the snow, casting green and sickly shadows.

Even Hailey looks off in this light, especially when she turns to me and waits for an answer.

We've flown so far tonight, and I thought it was all good. Quiet and safe, a brand-new beginning. As we coasted dark hills and blind descents, I let Hailey keep her hand. Instead, I caressed her ear and the curve of her neck; I smoothed over the round of her shoulder and flitted my touch against her knee. I felt so brave, all flavors of bold, and I still feel that way in spite of her question.

"Yeah," I say, certain this is true. "Everything's great. Why?"

Scooping a hand beneath mine, Hailey holds me in place. "You seem distracted."

Do I? Am I? It's been a long, weird day. It's been the beginning and end of time, all closed up in this day. But this, now, is good. I packed my boxes tight before I got in her car again.

Alone with her, miles and miles away from our real lives, this is paradise. The clouds burned off before sunset; the moon is so fat and bright, it looks like a lie.

If we weren't parked in this god-awful gas station, we could make out all the stars. Make out under the Milky Way; let the galaxy turn and turn behind us, infinity small and cold next to the heat we make.

But if Hailey notices something, one of those boxes came open, obviously. My insides need no poking, no prodding. My brains spit out excuses like ticker tape, long threads of it doubling back in case some explanation isn't enough.

"Syd's still being weird," I say.

Hailey rubs her lips together. Her gaze skims across my face; it flickers from brows to lips, lingering. She's weighted with import and thought; she rubs the back of my gloved hand with her thumb. When she lifts her head, I feel her focus change. It climbs the silver ladder of the scar, right up to my eye. "Can I ask you something?"

Oh god. There it is.

I don't mean to sigh, but I do. I haven't been waiting for her to ask about the scar, exactly, but I'm not shocked that she finally is. What's weird is that I don't want to tell her.

Because everybody already knows.

My Girl Scout troop, their parents, the newspaper, the local TV station, probably everybody I went to grade school with, most of middle school. Not all of high school because we got fed into the place out of a couple small towns when some district lines changed.

But Hailey's from Walker's Corner, just like I am.

She already knows. She has to. She didn't just grow up in a random cop's house; she grew up with Matthew Cho. Who was there. Who knows. Who kept her working a desk at the police station until just this summer probably *because* of the knowing. But she's gonna ask anyway, and I hate it. There should be better thoughts in Hailey's head, sweeter dreams, no nightmares. No poison.

Before I get a chance to say any of that, Hailey goes on. "Like, were you and Syd a thing?"

"I—What?"

The cackle that escapes me sounds unhinged. Not what I expected her to ask, obviously. Not a thought I ever expected in my head. I'm so stupidly, giddily relieved that I fall back against my seat.

Hailey looks hurt, so I squeeze her hand. Probably she thinks I'm laughing at *her*, instead of in the face of destiny. Quickly I reassure her. "We're just friends. Since we were little kids, that's it."

"Huh. She said she'd break me if I hurt you." She puts air quotes around the words "break me."

Surprise springs up like the flame on a birthday candle. It's not that I can't hear Syd saying something like that. When we were stuck learning square dancing in eighth-grade gym, Scott Caldwell kept letting his palm slip up her back and under her bra strap. Finally, she told him if he did it again, she'd break off his hand and shove it down his throat. So yeah, that's absolutely reasonable in Syd-realm.

I twist in the seat so I can look Hailey in the eye. "She's just being protective. I've never . . ."

Gently Hailey prompts, "Never what?"

"Gone out with anyone. Done any of this. Before."

"Wait." Hailey softens, covering our joined hands with her free one. Her voice softens, too, velvety on my skin. The corners of her lips turn up. It's not quite a smile; it's tempered and curious. Everything about the way she moves changes the air around us. Instead of cold and thin and tense, it's newly bright, like the edge of spring. "*Any* of this? Was I your first kiss?"

I blush, tingling from the static tension between us. "Yes. Is that bad?"

"Noooo." Hailey slides closer, near enough to kiss. "It's sweet. You should have told me."

"I'm kind of glad you couldn't tell." I don't know why, but she makes it easy to be—more. More the self I want to be: fearless and easy and even relaxed. Funny is probably going way too far, but I like the joking and teasing that happen when we're alone.

Hailey catches me up in a brand-new kiss. On first taste, it's sweet, her lips feathering against mine Then it ignites. Hunger burns on the tip of my tongue. Our breath falls hard and fast and in time.

We're breathing each other, devouring each other. The windows slowly rise with a haze. Releasing my seat belt, I slide back against the door when Hailey washes over me.

Her heat, her weight, erase everything. I'm not numb; I'm alive in a whole new way. A ceaseless, sensual way that makes it easy to wrap my arms around her. The front seats are narrow, so we have to hold on. We have to twist together—duck and dodge and slide back in for another deep taste.

This time, we fit together perfectly. Hailey's hands fall in the right places, my skin rising in chills of delight in their wake. When I venture beneath the hem of her sweater, I dip fingers beneath her waistband, stroking the dimples at the base of her spine. She is creamy; her kiss swirls in me like I'm coffee, around and around until she's mine and I'm hers and there's no way to separate us.

On the floor, my bag starts buzzing. I set it to vibrate; no idea who it is and right now, it's not important. Hailey's lips, blushed and full, those are what's important. When she breaks away, I chase her, begging for another taste, pleading for one, getting one.

Her hair escapes its elastic and falls all around us. Each strand leaves a mark on me. With a shake of her head to get it out of the way, she presses me back again.

I love that we're in the middle of nowhere. That we're in a car, like it's 1956 and Lovers' Lane is a thing. That we're right on the edge of one country and could tip over into another with ease.

She moves, and it's delicious. When she strokes my face, the muscles in her back ripple all the way down. Chasing that wave, I rasp my nails against her spine and savor the shiver that rolls through her. The phone buzzes again, and Hailey murmurs, right on my lips, "Should you get that?"

When I reply, my tongue flickers against the part of her lips. "No, it's fine."

"Are you sure?" she asks.

This time, I dip more than my fingertips beneath the band of her leggings. She makes a soft sound, and I pull her tighter against me. I want to fit all our curves and edges together, seamlessly. My lips feel heavy, honeyed, and I kiss her chin, her cheek, the corner of her mouth. "So sure."

So sure, and I'm not sure if the phone vibrates again after that.

I DO NOT GET HOME AT TEN.

It's 12:42 when I slink in the front door, and I really, really think I'm going to get to sneak to my bedroom and call it a night. I'm kiss drunk and love stoned, obviously. But I don't need to explain all that to—

Oh no. There's a light on in the kitchen.

After I shut the front door, the dead bolt latching sounds like a prison scene in the movies: *chunk-chunk*. Wincing at the sound, I freeze in place when my mother calls my name.

She also called six times while I was with Hailey. *Six*.

For a second, I seriously consider saying nothing. I'm two years old again. If I can't see you, you can't see me. Ridiculous.

"Come here," my mother calls. She has to raise her voice so I can hear her, and that blunts the tone in it. Is she merely annoyed, or is she furiously angry? Only one way to find out.

I peel out of my coat and take the long, dread walk to the kitchen. It's hard to pre-construct arguments when I've so clearly screwed up. I try, though. I have check boxes in my head.

Pleading to the past: this has never happened before, therefore

I swear it will never happen again. Pleading to my character: I'm a good kid who doesn't get in trouble, therefore this is fine. Pleading to her good nature: I was having so much fun, and lost track of time, and doesn't she want me to go out more?

What takes me aback when I hit the kitchen door isn't so much the look on Mom's face as the color of it. Most of the time, she has a golden, summery shade about her. Her cinnamon freckles make her look way younger than she is. With thick lashes and perfectly pink lips, she looks like she's wearing makeup even when she isn't.

But there's no summer here. She sits at the island in our kitchen with a cup of coffee and a face as grey as slate. With all her color gone and her expression scrubbed down to a sheer, impenetrable expanse, I'm suddenly afraid someone has died.

"This," my mother says, curling her hands around her cup. "Is not acceptable. How many times did I call you?"

All of my special pleadings fly out of my head. Instead, I bleat out, "We lost track of time."

My mother's fingers dance on the edge of her cup. Her nails tink against ceramic, little warnings that I can't translate but I understand. She's never been a yeller. (She's never had to be. My wings were clipped early, and I like school, so what's to yell about?) She takes a beat, just a second of silence. "What, exactly, is going on with you?"

"Nothing," I say, offended. What a lie.

"It's clearly something. This past week, you've been up all night—out all night. I know you took my car, Ava."

All over, I'm slapped with a guilty flush. Rubbing my heel

against the floor, I don't meet my mother's eyes. Even I can't justify a lie about the car. I did take it; drove through the night in it. Went to see Jane in it; crashed into Nick because of it. There's literally nothing I can say to save myself from that, although hilariously, I think, *If you only knew* why *I took the car, Mother.*

Mom taps her mug again. "Well?"

Selectively, I carve up my time. I hack it to pieces and stitch it back together, Frankenstein's truth. Curling my arms on the island, I slump before her and look up through my bangs at her. Supplicant, pleading. "It was stupid."

"Obviously."

"I just . . . Mom. I really like her. And she really likes me. And I thought it would be romantic to, like, show up at her window in the middle of the night. And I shouldn't have done it. I was scared the whole way home, I promise. It was so stupid, and I'll never do it again."

Gathering herself, Mom takes a deep breath. It's like she's charging up to blast me. "You're right; it'll never happen again. Next time, I'll call the police."

That threat—that promise—is a bucket of ice water dumped over me. Would she really? It's not like I want to find out, but I sort of want to find out. I think it's the strongest weapon she has, and she'd never use it. I think.

My nod is staggered, up and down, wobbling sideways. I swear, "I will never, never do it again, Mom."

"Is that the whole thing?" she asks. She clarifies, "Is that what all of this has been about, this week? Chasing this girl?"

Uh-oh. Instantly I reverse. If Hailey becomes the Bad Influence, I'll never get to see her again. "No. No. I mean, yes, I've been hanging out with her a lot. I—I like her a lot. But Syd is going through some stuff, and I'm trying to help her. . . ."

"I'm not a monster," Mom informs me. "If you want to go on a date—"

"Nobody goes on dates anymore, Mom."

Her eyebrow shoots up. "Is this really the time and place for semantics?"

I shrink back. "No."

"Like I said, if you want to go on a date, that's great. I'm happy for you! I'm glad to see you getting out a little bit. But you're not an adult, Ava. You don't make your schedule; you don't make your curfew. I do."

"Okay, okay," I say. Haven't I apologized enough? Am I doing it wrong or something?

"And these are the rules." Mom flips her phone over; her lockscreen is a picture of me in these big round sunglasses, giving her a cheesy grin. She saw the sunnies at the gas station and bought them on a whim. They're bug-eyed and strange and hilarious, and it's so weird that that's the picture she wants to see of me, every day.

My phone pings: a text. I open it and there is, honest to god, a list of new rules right there. While I was making out with Hailey at the edge of the world, my mother was sitting home in the dark writing a new covenant for our house. I slipped the cage, and now she's rebarring it.

1. *Curfew on school nights is 9:30.*
2. *Curfew on weekends is 10:00.*
3. *I expect you to be home on school nights. No sleepovers.*
4. *I expect you to ASK PERMISSION before going out.*
5. *If your grades slip, there will be consequences.*
6. *You will take your driver's test within 60 days.*
7. *You will not drive my car without me present, ever.*
8. *You will answer the phone when I call.*
9. *Common sense is the rule.*

After I skim the list, I look up at her. "Common sense?"

My mother stands. "You're not just a smart girl, Ava. You're brilliant. I expect you to know what I would and would not want you doing, and to act accordingly."

No tattoos, no dead girls in the woods, no stalking killers, no meeting strangers for coffee, no driving to Canada, no climbing fire towers, no speeding through the dark of night with the girl I like, no sleeping in her bed and waking up to her face instead of the sun.

No to this whole past week. No to anything that terrifies me or creates me or makes me over into a whole new Ava. No to all the things that push the borders of my little, little world even an inch further out. No changing my map. My map remains the same.

There's a knot in my throat, and the ice maker on the fridge grumbles for me. It looks like Mom's going to go to bed. That was her mic drop, but I don't let it hit the floor. I say, "Are you just mad that I finally got a life?"

Apparently, this was exactly the wrong response. Until now she's been annoyed but, like, vaguely human. Now her eyes go flat and dark like a shark's, and her shoulders rise like bat's wings. Nighttime cuts her into angles, and she clenches her jaw.

"You're grounded," she says flatly. And then, like I'm six and naughty, she jerks her head toward the stairs. "Go to bed."

She turns her back on me. She waits for me to walk away. This isn't fair. This isn't her. But when I don't immediately move under her command, she flicks her thumb across the screen of her phone and says, "Now."

I wonder what happens if I don't.

I only wonder.

I'm not that brave.

WHAT LITTLE SLEEP I GET FEELS STOLEN.

It's snatches of time where I might be dreaming or I might be awake. Where my mother's clenched jaw and Nick's mechanical voice somehow blend into bad dreams that aren't quite nightmares.

Morning is still black; it comes on the back of an alarm and the sensation that I'm just giving up and getting out of bed, rather than waking. The weight of days, of disaster, tries to drag me back to bed. Everything is screwed up—everything except being with Hailey. And that's gonna blow as soon as she finds out—

I shut up my head with vicious self-talk: *I'm stupid, nobody else would end up in this position. It's just me, flawed me, top of her class and still failing at life. No matter what, I have to go to school today. I don't know what grounded* is *yet. I just feel certain it will be monumentally worse if I screw up today.*

This time, I barely turn down the heat at all. I scald myself in the shower. And when I step out, there she is. Lark. Her outline isn't so certain anymore. She's a maiden in the mist, a hazy shade made of steam and too little sleep. When I open the shower curtain, she swirls in eddies, invisible currents, then coalesces again.

Not this. I don't have time for this. There's a plan; I'll hear from Nick soon. Lark is not here. She's in her grave; in the woods. She's away. Elsewhere. Not *not* here. This time I won't be tempted down to the river. That was before. That was . . . fantasy. Delusion. Something.

I wrap one towel around my body and drop another on my head. Sightless, I scrub my skin dry, hard, till it burns. I can't see her, but now she whispers, so close she should be touching me.

"Answer your phone," she says.

It's not ringing, and I don't owe a hallucination an explanation. I will not listen; I will not answer. Yanking the towel from my head, I yelp. There, in the mirror, J— Lark—

Battered and beaten. A blackened, bloody stripe painted across her empty eyes. Blood mats her hair, and the deep, V-shaped gouge in her breast has turned black around the edges. This is not the girl who looked through my window or watched from the corner.

This is the body in the woods, the bella in the wych elm, the corpse that's rotting even though I'd like to pretend it's not. Her lips move, soundless. But I can read what they say.

Answer your phone.

A coward, I turn away from the mirror. And there's Lark, swimming in the mist again. She drifts around me like smoke, her eyes plaintive. But her mouth twists. Angry. This isn't a ghost; this is a revenant. She comes back for a reason; she'll stop at nothing.

Syd once told me that people who are crazy don't think they're crazy. I told her you can't say "crazy" like mental illness is all one thing. It's not, but I have to admit that right now, there's definitely something wrong with my brain, because ghosts aren't real.

The face rotting in my mirror isn't real.

The face accusing in the steam isn't real.

I throw open the bathroom door. Cold air rushes in. It burns off heat like daybreak burns off fog. The mirror rolls with condensation, and I try to dry my stupid hair without looking up from my feet. Panic heart sets in: something tight wrapped around it, beating painfully fast against it.

This is my imagination. It has *been* my imagination. From the moment I found her body in the woods, anxiety and trauma and fear and stress have turned my brain into a midnight carnival. The music is bloated with a minor key, and everything shifts like in a fun house mirror.

"Ava," Lark says. Then her voice doubles, two speaking at once. "Ava, answer the phone."

"It's not ringing!" I yell. In the far reaches of the house, I think I hear my mother move. She shouldn't be here. It's past time for her to be gone, but if she's here, she can—

What? Bring down the ban hammer a little harder? She can't do anything. She never did anything. *Pray she's gone, girl. Get yourself together!*

I flee the bathroom, my own bathroom, in my own room, in my own house. Throwing open my closet door, I strangle a scream.

Lark hangs there, her head tilted at an unnatural angle.

"Your phone is ringing," she says behind me.

I shriek and whip around. There's nothing behind me, and my phone sits in the middle of my bed where I threw it! It's dark;

the clock is even dimmed on the lockscreen. No notifications, no nothing.

I slam the door and dig into my dresser instead. Socks, underwear, bra, cami, black fleece leggings, black oversized sweater, on, on, on, I just throw my clothes on so I can get out of here. No jewelry today, no makeup, none of it, just get out.

Grabbing my phone and my bag, I sprint out of my own bedroom. My feet crash hard on the steps, and I slide on the landing. Skidding into the kitchen, I'm not even sure where I think I'm going. (Not thinking, just running.) It's a good thing I'm alone in this house—

I'm not.

Lark is there, elbows propped on the island. She's waiting for an answer. She taps her fleshless fingertips on the counter. Bone on slate, drumming a march.

"Just calm down," I tell myself aloud.

Somewhere, far away ago, there was a school counselor who kept butterscotches on her desk and let me sit in the beanbag nest in the corner of her office. She told me when things were too big or too scary that it was okay to talk to myself. Just say, *It's all right. I'm safe here.* I know that was After Him, but I don't remember if it was Because of Him.

Calm down, calm down, calm down, I think. I open the fridge to grab a Pepsi and slam it shut again instantly. It's full of blood. It's stuffed full of a body. Lark's body, nude and degraded, wrecked and desecrated, fills the whole space.

When I slam it shut, every bottle inside the door crashes.

That's going to be a mess, how am I going to explain that mess, how am I going to put myself back together again when there's a dead girl in my house and she won't stop saying, "Answer the phone, Ava"?

It's not ringing. It's NOT ring—

It's ringing.

I'M OUTSIDE OF ME, AND I SEE THAT I'M FROZEN. My hand clutches the door handle inside an unfamiliar car. My forehead presses against the cold glass of the window. I sit there in layers upon layers; I realize I'm wearing two pairs of underpants again.

Nick's car smells . . . bad. Not like body odor. Like aftershave and sweat; like the gym after the basketball team has its extra day practices. Crumpled burger wrappers festoon the back seat, little floral points of interest on top of a backpack and a stripe of duct tape holding the pleather together.

Even though the heater blasts, threaded with the pungent scent of oil or antifreeze from the engine, I shiver. We are on our way to the cop's house. The house where Nick thinks Lark died. My throat is so dry; I just want something to drink. My stomach is so tight; it twists in sour knots.

"Explain to me how we know he's not home?" I ask. It feels like asking for a bedtime story. A fairy tale: enchanted words that will make everything right with the world.

"Smart ssssecurity system n-not very . . . smart."

He hands me the tablet crammed between our seats, waving a hand. He can't really drive and talk at the same time. Instead, he lets me look—again. It's creepy that I can sit in a moldering Toyota Corolla, easily doing seventy on the highway, and watch the insides of someone's house.

Thumbnails of each room nestle in the app's toolbar. I touch one, and there's an empty kitchen. It seems like a still photo until a cat walks through the doorway, its tail pointed at the ceiling. The whole house is wired; I can watch two different empty beds, the inside of an empty garage, an empty living room. It's a digital dollhouse waiting to be filled with people.

We hit town, and Nick slows to a crawl. Tourist trap towns like Walker's Corner are known for two things: an ox load of kitsch and extremely aggressive cops with ticket quotas. As we glide through a barely woken Main Street, my heart pounds irregularly. It's so hard to take a breath; every breath in this car makes my skin crawl.

Could I be having a heart attack? I press my fist in the middle of my sternum. It doesn't make the pounding stop; it just diffuses the ache. A sour pricking rises in my mouth when Nick turns at the candle shop. This is the road to Amber's tattoo studio. This is a road I've been on a million times.

We glide right past her warehouse loft; instead of left, we turn right. My head explodes with alarms. I've been here before; I've been in this alley. I've seen that fence from the outside.

Without a word, Nick throws the car into park, then reaches for the tablet. His fingers fly, swift across the screen. And then the lights outside this house go off. Hazy morning darkness surrounds us. It's not pitch but dim. I spill out of the car onto the drive.

What if there are dogs? Vicious dogs? What if there's a secret basement? What ifwhatifwhatifwhatif?! But if Nick has reservations, they don't show. His spine is straight; his step, sure. When we reach the back door, he goes to the tablet again.

All he has to do is draw a finger along a slide, and the red light on the back-door lock turns green. He nods at me to open it. I'm the one wearing gloves. Wincing, I push it open. No alarms blare. The cat doesn't even streak out the door between our legs.

The house just opens, abracadabra. Some citrusy scent greets us from the kitchen. We're in the kitchen; the clock on the microwave ticks over from 6:39 to 6:40. A grumble startles me. It's just the ice maker in the fridge resetting. Ours does it too.

I follow Nick, because he seems to know where he's going. How much time has he spent watching them secretly through their own cameras? Does he watch them sleep? Has he seen them stripped for a shower when they thought they were alone? My innards recoil at that thought. Being seen, vulnerable and ignorant, through the system that's supposed to keep them safe.

But if Lark's killer lives here, he doesn't deserve to be safe.

He doesn't deserve to watch the playoffs in one of those La-Z-Boys in the living room. He doesn't deserve nice meals in that kitchen; he shouldn't get comfort and care and warmth and happiness. He deserves none of that. Tick by tick, righteous anger melts away my anxiety.

Down a long wallpapered hallway lies our destination.

A bedroom, crammed tight with a bed too big for the space. Walls obscured by posters of half-naked women and half-million-dollar cars. Lotion on the headboard, mountains of clothes on the floor. This room is musky and feral, and I don't want to be trapped in it.

Nick goes straight for the laptop in the middle of the bed. I wouldn't touch that comforter in a hazmat suit, but he sits down like he's at home. As he rifles through this guy's digital bedroom, I'm stuck looking through the real thing.

I have a list on my phone; Nick texted me before he picked me up. Lark's necklace is missing: a half-moon charm with a blue stone in it, delicate on a silver chain. A snake ring, one that climbs the finger, its silver tongue lapping at the knuckles. Her wallet, her ID—the things he didn't find in the dumpster.

As Nick takes pictures of the laptop screen, I kick through the crap on the floor. I hate this. I hate this room. I hate everything about it. And what I hate most is that Lark might have spent her last night on earth in here.

I freeze when I kick over some jeans to reveal a plaid shirt. It looks just like the one she wore when I saw her on the side of the road.

(basket case)

But when I kick it over, I realize it's not a shirt at all. It's a bandana or something, with a screen-printed band logo. My head pounds as the adrenaline ebbs briefly. Turning in the narrow space, I edge around the bed to his side tables. They have drawers, and they're piled high with all kinds of garbage.

There's an ashtray overflowing and another ashtray full of change, not so overflowing. I don't care that I'm wearing gloves; I don't want to touch anything. I use the edge of a magazine to move things aside. Two empty Mountain Dew cans topple, exposing a bottle of Tylenol—and a necklace.

A silver necklace with a half-moon charm on it.

Claws clutch at my heart. That's proof. That's *evidence* she was here. Lark was here, alone, with this guy, and who takes off a necklace when they're just sitting around and visiting? I mean, who even takes off a necklace when they're hooking up? I lean down to get a better look: the chain is broken.

"Nick," I whisper. I point.

His grim expression darkens. He mimes a finger on a camera. *Take a picture*, the gesture says. I do, but I have to take it three times because my hands shake. This is real, this is really real, and she stood here, she was hurt here, she was taken apart—here. I'm standing in the last traces of her life. I'm the heat that drains from her body.

A screaming whirlwind of crows fills my head. This whole house shifts around me. It closes in. This too-full room is too tight. The orange freshness smells like the dust they drop on vomit at school.

Through tears, I take more pictures of the necklace. I fight every muscle in my body to stay still. My skin wants to peel off; my bones will run away if I let them. What have I done? How I did I end up here?

"Look sharp."

My neck crackles when I whip around to look. The windows are still dark, and Lark frames herself in them. She's a horror, but her voice is an urgent bell. Her head rolls onto her shoulder as she gestures toward the outside.

"He's coming."

I SNATCH THE TABLET OFF THE BED, AND SHE'S right. There's a truck in front of the house. Its headlights linger, and a slender silhouette of a man approaches the front door. I can't see his face. That doesn't matter. He belongs here; I don't. We don't.

Too hard, I grab Nick's arm and shake him. I shove the tablet under his nose, and then I whisper, "We have to get out of here."

Now we're both live wires. Nick takes a couple more pictures and then rolls off the bed. He's fast (I already knew that) faster than me (knew that, too). He reaches back into the room and grabs me. I don't know how we're going to get out.

This place is a ranch, one long hallway, basically. Burning, I turn in place until Nick puts his hands on me again. They're hard and alien and his grip crushes when he drags me backward into the bathroom. I start to flail. It's a reflex; his arms tight around me. The stink of his aftershave. *Nonononono,* screams in my heart and my blood and my brains.

"Let go of me," I growl, elbowing back against him. "Let go!"

He releases me and hisses. I think he's trying to say, *Shut up,* but he just can't get past the "shhhhh." His breath still falls on the back of my neck. It's a tiny bathroom, doesn't even have a tub. We're trapped.

We're trapped, we're trapped.

Footsteps fall in the hallway. The cat casts out a greeting yowl. And behind me, there's a metallic click. This is a cop's house! This is a killer's house! What do cops and killers have in common?!

Gun. He has a gun.

Instantly, I act. This won't be for nothing. I'm gonna lean into it. A dead girl led me here. A dead girl warned me to get out. I'm not gonna let her down. Whatever happens next, to me, maybe I deserve it. But she didn't. All she did was meet up with a boy who turned out to be a beast.

Turning, I yank off my backpack and unzip it. I shove in the tablet and my phone. I tell Nick, low and close to his face, "Your phone, put it in there. Put everything in there!"

He hesitates, baffled. I point past him, to the small window above the toilet. *Throw the backpack out*, I say with a glare. Backpack first! If we get caught, and get

(killed)

arrested, the evidence is still there. It's still safe.

Thank god, Nick finally gets it without me saying anything else. We don't have time for anything else. He dumps a couple of things into the bag.

Then he steadies me when I step up on the toilet and push out the screen. It makes the worst noise when it hits the ground. Like throwing spoons into a garbage disposal or something. But

I throw the bag after it.

Hopefully, it lands somewhere hidden. I don't know. I can't see.

"Aroostook County Sheriff," a man's voice rings out. "I know you're in there!"

The cop. It's the cop. A relief and a terror at the same time.

I go to step down, and Nick shakes his head. Now he points. So hard that his elbow pops, he points at me, then the window. He thinks I can fit. He thinks I should run.

A warm rush floods me; yes, yes, run. Run away, run as fast as you can, but that's a gingerbread man. A fairy tale. And I don't have time for those anymore.

I jump from the toilet and press in close to him. "You're on probation. Get the backpack and run."

He shakes his head, and in reply, I shove him toward the window. It's not a negotiation. It's not a question. It's not a request. He gets out, and hopefully, I get out alive too.

In the hallway, the footsteps stop right outside the bathroom door. A brief, three-note digital tone tells us everything. Whoever's on the other side just called 911.

Before I knew she was Lark, I promised Jane I would take care of her. I promised I'd protect her. Knowing her name doesn't change that. In fact, it sharpens it. By god, I made promises, and I'm gonna keep them.

I shove Nick toward the window again. Hard. He's gonna fall, or he's gonna leave.

In a surprising feat of agility, he leaps up, shimmies through, and he's gone.

I pull the curtains closed, then I step toward the bathroom door. On wobbly legs, I try to stand tall and straight and certain. It takes two tries to get my throat to give up its sound. When it finally does, I call out, "Don't hurt me. I'll come out. Just please don't hurt me."

"Put your hands up," he barks from the other side.

Raising my hands, I squeeze my eyes closed, and I hope this is the part where I get arrested. Just arrested. God, what is my life?

Abruptly, the thin door swings open. It bounces against the wall, and I try not to shake when the man in a sheriff's uniform levels his gun in my direction. It's dull and black, like a void.

"There's a dead girl in the woods," I say suddenly. As I do, I catch a glimpse of Lark in the bathroom mirror. She fades, she fades, and then—

She's gone.

I DON'T REMEMBER A LOT FROM THE IN BETWEEN? From Before? With the Summer Man?

I'm in the middle of this storm with Lark's murder, and I think probably in a year or two or six, I won't remember this middle part, either.

This time, there are no detectives. Not right away.

The man on the other side of the bathroom door is a sheriff's deputy, and he is *pissed.* I burst into tears. His voice sounds like thunder. I know it's questions—what body, what woods, what does that have to do with anything—but I can't even breathe. I can't answer.

Because I won't (can't) say why I'm in there, he holsters the gun furiously. He makes me sit on the toilet until the *other* cops arrive.

I don't say anything to them, either, but they don't seem to care. They talk on their shoulder mics: breaking and entering, robbery, body, lies—whatever, they don't care. They're gonna process me, and this'll be a whole new adventure compared to the last time.

(Nobody got arrested last time.)

A camera flashes me blind again, and this time, there's a mug shot. Mine. Fingerprints, too, where I roll my fingers on a scanner one at a time, then wait for a beep.

It's almost beautiful, the loops and whorls of my identity in black and white. It's like living forever in π, which contains every number, every thread: your social security number, your birthday, your address, your DNA sequence, your favorite book in binary.

Now I'm twice contained by the police. I have a victim folder. (Though that was probably shredded a long time ago; if my rape kit remains, it probably hasn't been tested. Probably won't ever be tested.) And they take my meager things and put them in envelopes. To wit, I am:

(1) ring, silver
(1) nose stud, diamond.

Nothing else. Because the rest is in the backpack. The rest is—god, I hope—in Nick's hands, and hopefully he's talking to a lawyer who's gonna talk to the police or something or somebody. Hopefully, he's not going to leave me in jail. Hopefully, hopefully, ha ha ha: what a stupid, useless word.

I believe he'll come, because I have to believe it.

The cops have to take my word for it about my identity, because I have no ID with me. They look askance when I tell them I'm seventeen—

(underage! minor! alert!)

and I don't know how this would *usually* go, but they put me in a small cell with a concrete bench and leave me alone for a long time. Long enough that I get to read the graffiti etched into the walls (I wonder with what, because I couldn't leave a mark here if I wanted to). Long enough that I'm sure I've been noted absent at school. Long enough that my mom is gonna get a robocall from Attendance annnny minute now, telling her I'm not there.

Maybe all that time gone is why the guard (officer? matron? I have no idea) finally unlocks the door and leads me to a desk. Asks for the number I want to call as she holds an institutional phone halfway between the desk and her ear.

Sure, I consider calling Syd or Hailey. But those thoughts drain away silently. One is gone; the other will be soon, I'm sure. And anyway, the only number I know by heart is my mother's.

(I would have picked her anyway.

Probably.

I guess we'll never know.)

I know that I tell her I've been arrested, and I know that I ask her to come help me. But I swear, her responses are only silence. Long pauses. They probably aren't. I think there are words; I'm sure there's anger. But I just have nothing in me to hear; I'm not in me, not really.

It's a quiet kind of numb, a shock that doesn't sting. It just vibrates. I need my mom because I need to tell her about Lark. I need her to find out from *me* that I'm not in jail because I decided to take up recreational trespassing. I need her to tell me what to do.

Because I am well past being protected now. Mom can't keep

me in the tower. The only thing she can do is stand with me or turn away from me. Something Terrible has happened before, and she's the one who stood. Who stayed. I'm pretty sure she'll do it again. I think. I wish. I

(hope).

When I hand the phone back to the GuardMatronLady, she doesn't take me back to the cell. Instead, she walks me up a hall and deposits me in a small cold room. It's outfitted with a big mirror wall, a plain bolted-down table, and two chairs. The walls are a scuffed, institutional green, and I'm sure people watch me from the other side of that glass.

All I see is myself, with hollowed-out eyes and fried hair and greyed skin. I burrow into my own arms. What's funny—funny peculiar, not funny ha-ha—is that I think I look a lot like Nick looked that night in the Red Stripe. Back when he was hoping his camera full of evidence would magically reappear at the Customer Service desk. I guess we've been careening down the same train tracks, toward the same brick wall, for a while now, he and I.

When the door opens, I expect Detective Cho.

(Because of course! Because why not?! I know everything with Hailey is definitely over now. Because there's no way the father who only finally let her get a library job *this year* is ever going to let his little girl go out with a felon.

God, everything is over. Syd is over. Hailey is over. My *life* is over.)

A swish of perfume precedes the detective. It's not Detective Cho; it's a Black woman with coiled braids and a mask for an expression. Her badge sits comfortably at her waist. She's got a gun belt under her jacket, which matches her dress pants and sensible shoes.

"Ava, right?" she asks, looking at a folder.

What could possibly be in it? All I am is a girl who got caught in somebody else's house. Did they somehow dig up my past? Will it count for or against me? I almost want her to ask about the scar. *Ask. Ask about it, Detective.*

She goes to shake my hand. "I'm Detective Pera. How are you? Can I get you anything?"

The way she asks sets my teeth on edge. I don't think it's a real question—like, if I asked for a cup of coffee, she'd probably say something like, "Lemme get a few things down here, and then we can get that coffee for you."

"My mom. I'm only seventeen."

"She's on her way," she tells me. "But we can talk until she gets here, right?"

So patronizing. I'm already a liar to her. A criminal. Fair enough. I've done a really shady thing. No, I've done a lot of shady things and told a lot of lies and acted so screwed up that I look guilty.

And I am guilty; I stalked a guy. I broke into a house. I hid Lark's body.

The body thing might not even be against the law, but trailing Nick, downloading his whole phone, attacking him in the woods? Those parts are definitely a few different levels of illegal. Breaking into a house; getting caught inside it: so illegal.

Not to mention all the forbidden ink I wear on my skin.

There are layers and layers to peel here. Nobody's going to cry, because this isn't an onion. I'm an old, moldering scroll crushed between sheets of oxidized bronze. It's going to take a specialist to figure out everything inside me.

I wrap my arms around myself and say, "I'm gonna wait for her."

"Hey," Detective Pera says gently. "All we're trying to do is figure out what's going on. You said something about a body? That sounds pretty scary."

She sounds so seductively reasonable. My forebrain wants to tell her everything, but my lizard brain hisses for me to *stop, stop, stop. Just shut up. Say nothing.*

I know for a fact that I have a right to remain silent. Miranda versus Arizona was decided in 1966, exactly nine hundred years after William of Normandy added "the Conqueror" to his name and took over Britain.

Detective Pera allows herself to look a little annoyed when I shake my head. "How am I supposed to help you if you won't let me?"

Because she doesn't know, she has to ask. Cajole. Maybe if I were Nick, she'd even yell. But I've learned some things this past week. People can't look at you and know what's in your head. In your heart. In the moment.

They overlook everything except the things we say out loud, explicitly. And that means, if we say nothing, they move on in their own orbits and spheres and galaxies.

We're all just shells filled with secrets and lies and words we never say. I don't smile; instead, I ask, "Can I have something to drink?"

Her chair grinds against the floor when she pushes it back. "Do you know Deputy Sheriff Pelletier?"

With full and complete honesty, I can say, "No."

"What about *Zach* Pelletier?"

I press my lips together and shake my head. *Mm mm, no. Nope.* I don't, at all, but I *do* wonder if that's the guy in those Discord chats, the OhWeeOh that ArcanePriestess was supposed to meet up with that night. But that's *my* question, *my* secret stash. I'm not giving it up.

Tipping her head to one side, Detective Pera considers me. Her eyes are still a mystery, but I know what's behind them. She wants answers for a break-in . . . but the body. I said I knew where a body was. Maybe she *is* on my side. Maybe she *is* worried there's a dead girl in the woods, that I'm keeping in my soul.

But just like it's impossible to look into me and to know, I don't see anything in Detective Pera's eyes. Maybe all she wants is *I lied, I'm a juvenile delinquent, I broke in, and this is why*, on video, audio, preserved and ready for court.

Her voice is measured when she says, trying to come across as sincere, "From what I can tell, you're a good kid. There's gotta be an explanation for this, Ava."

Changed the subject, didn't she? My mind's already a mixed-up, screwed-up, goat's breakfast of a thing, and she's trying to mess with it. For Lark's sake, I'm glad that Detective Pera's going to be working on her murder. But for me? I want her to listen, to hear, when I say I'm not saying anything until my mom arrives.

This is why I think I won't remember all this later. It's too much and too heavy. It's too scary and too alien. It's a place I never wanted to be, and a moment I hope won't scar me until the end of days. That's why I told you everything that came before. And I'll tell you what comes after, as best as I can.

But this part here, I'm going to put it in a box. An iron box, with iron bands. An iron lock and a key I'll throw away. This box will sink to the bottom of my ocean, and I'll never, ever open it again. Because what happens in the police station doesn't actually matter, but it's the part where I have to realize:

A bad thing happened to me. And it's still happening.

But I ended up *here* all on my own.

MY MOTHER COMES IN LIKE A NOR'EASTER.

Her voice, howling and furious, precedes her. She spits out consonants like hail, which means I can make out the most important words long before I see her. *Underage. Child. Lawyer. Charges. No.*

And then, right outside the door, she says, "We'll see about *that.*"

Then she sweeps into the room. I don't think she even let the detective open the door for her. One minute she's out, then she's in, roaring around me, until I'm in the calm circle of her eye. Her hands fall on my shoulders. She stands behind me, and I see her eyes flicker briefly in the mirror.

The tattoos.

She has no idea I have tattoos until this moment. One eyebrow twitches. To me, it's a sign set on fire in the middle of the night, visible for miles. Still, she turns back to Detective Pera. "I need a moment with my daughter. Alone."

And then, proving either that she's picked up a lot of stuff from the firm she works at or that she, too, watches television, she points at the mirror. "And if somebody's listening on the other side, they'd better shut the sound off now. We want a lawyer."

Detective Pera doesn't roll her eyes. But she does shut the door harder than she needs to. Mom waits a few seconds, giving the glass a hard glare. Then she pulls up the chair next to me. Forcibly turns my chair to face hers. Leans into my face and asks, under her breath, "What the hell is going on?"

Suddenly desperate, I grab for her hands. They're familiar but cold, because she hates wearing gloves. The rough spot on the back of her hand is the pin in a map I've read a million times.

Maybe these hands held me too tight; maybe they let me slip through at the worst possible moment. But they are home; they are my mother and my true north and I need to be a fixed point. Just for now. Just until the whole world shifts under me again.

"There's a dead girl in the woods, Mom."

Whole empires rise and fall in her eyes. I'll probably never know all the things she thinks at this exact moment. What she feels against what she knows, her heart against logic, but she's only wild for a moment. Something settles in her, hard. Her shoulders dip. She never lets go of my hands.

"You killed someone?"

"No, no no no!" I say, too loud, and she shushes me. Lowering my voice again, I say, "No, I *found* a body in the woods. I didn't hurt her, but I know who did. I have evidence. I have . . . proof."

And under my breath, I tell her everything because I'm probably going to jail and everything's going to come out anyway. I tell her about flying; about lying. About hunting Nick and Nick hunting me. The backpack in the bushes; the proof that Lark spent her last night alive with a guy who still has her necklace. Tattoos and Syd's anger and everything. Everything that feels relevant; everything I've told you.

I tell her about my friend Jane.

That I saw her. Talked to her. Lay in bed with her; answered the phone because of her. Mom gets greyer as I talk, but she doesn't interrupt. Doesn't move. Not until I finally shut up.

When I do, she shakes me. She actually puts her hands on my shoulders and shakes me. Not hard—strangely gentle, strangely plaintive. Her voice runs ragged, and she says, "You should have said something!"

"I know," I say. And then I break and press my brow to her shoulder. I can't weep; all my tears are gone. But wracking grief doesn't need tears to feed it. It wrenches through, completely on its own. It splits my breast and cracks my wishbone. I am crushed down to nothing.

You're not going to believe me when I say that most of the time I'm fine. Really. I do okay. I get by. But this isn't most of the time. In fact, I think it's safe to say that this is a singularity. What has happened now will never happen again, not in my life, not in history, not in the future.

So right now is not fine. I can't do this by myself. I look up at my mother and I say, "Mommy, I need help."

And she cries.

MY MOTHER DISAPPEARS, AFTER WARNING ME TO SAY nothing. She's gone forever, calling a lawyer, I think. I don't know. I don't care, really.

I curl my arms on the table and put my head down. Exhaustion is lead, poured into my skin. Honestly, if it weren't so bright in here, I think I could lie on the floor and sleep. I could slide right down, pull my sweatshirt over my face, and just sleep.

Rumpelstiltskin sleep, sleeping beauty slumber. Let the woods and the vines and the briars grow up around me.

Behind my closed eyes, I see Hailey. I see the streaks in her eyes and the ghost of freckles on her nose. The curve of her mouth and the drift of her hair, the way winter tugs it from beneath her hat. I wonder if she knows where I am

(that I've been arrested).

I wonder if she'll ever speak to me again, or if she'll just be silence. If the arrest is enough, no explanation needed. Then again, what explanation would ever, ever make sense to her? I can elaborate and justify and insist, but I cannot change an immutable fact—

Her dad is a cop. Has been her whole life. She probably goes to barbecues with his cop friends. This is the very station where she used to have a job (the one she was so excited to escape), and nothing bad, nothing tragic, nothing world-destroying has ever happened to her.

She has no reason to be afraid, she would never tremble at the prospect of talking to a detective.

In her head, there are no hospital room memories, no strange men upon strange men hovering, invading, lingering. That thought feels like a revelation. For a second, I'm almost outside myself, in Hailey's skin.

Yeah, she probably has a healthy sense of personal danger. There's no girl who walks through the world obliviously.

Somebody's told us to be careful, park under the lights, keep your keys between your fingers, carry pepper spray (but be careful because they can use pepper spray against you) or a stun gun (same) or a gun (nobody says watch out for the bad guy taking your gun, but that's a whole nother political issue, isn't it?) and cross the street if you have to but don't be on the street after dark.

Hailey moves through the world with a father who knows what kinds of bad things happen. She moves through the world aware of her surroundings, with ID when she leaves the house, and taking all necessary precautions because a girl in public is like a bag of gold. All kinds of people will do all kinds of things to get at treasure.

But all her fear is theoretical. I'm happy for her because of that, so happy, because I never want her to be afraid for *reasons*. I want joy for her and peace for her and sweet dreams for her, always. I'm glad she doesn't know. And at the same time, I am so *jealous*. It's a pang, a physical hunger—I want to believe the way she believes.

I just don't. I can't.

That's the thing the scar does. It's the line in the sand, between women who might become statistics and women who already are. I frighten people because I'm proof that bad things happen to people no matter what.

Already, I know people are going to say, "Well, look how Lark ended up." (If they remember her name.) Murdered, stuffed in a tree: that's what you get when you run away. (That's probably going to become her name: *That girl who was murdered in Maine, you know, the one they found stuffed inside a tree?*) That's what happens when you trust people you only know online.

But who in their right mind thinks we should hand out the death penalty for running away? For meeting people you've talked to for years?

I don't deserve a life sentence because of what he did to me, but I'm gonna serve one. The whisper of his memory is there with me—always.

If I'd never found Lark, I might have kept everything boxed forever. Worked around it. Gotten by. I might have spent my whole life hiding from myself and hating the scar that never let me hide completely.

I will always be the Ava I became because that man left his mark on me. But at least now I know—I can admit—I need help. I'm too far down to climb up on my own.

But let's not talk about me. Let's talk about you. (General you, not you in particular; I bet you're great.) Let's think about this. If you look at me and look at my scar and you shift uncomfortably in your seat—it's because you can't think of the reason why

You

will never be

Me.

DO YOU KNOW NICK CRENSHAW—

When the lawyer Mom hired asks me that, that's when I know things are about to change. I am half tremor and half puddle. He's the cavalry; he showed up just in time.

DO YOU KNOW LARK SUTTON—

That's her last name; she has a whole name: Lark Sutton. The girl with the Aquarius tattoo; the girl with the half-moon necklace. The girl; my Jane.

DO YOU KNOW ZACH PELLETIER—

Still don't. Never met him. Never want to. I know what happens to girls who meet him.

DO YOU RECOGNIZE THIS BACKPACK—

Of course I do. And I recognize the tablet and the phones in it. I recognize my school iPad and my wallet in it. I recognize every scrap of digital evidence in it. I recognize that this is the backpack that probably sends me to jail for breaking and entering (turns out it can't be burglary because I didn't take anything but pictures) but also condemns Lark's murderer to a cell for life. A life for a life; justice.

DO YOU RECOGNIZE THE AUTHORITY OF THIS COURT AND YOUR MOTHER—

I'm released to my mother's custody. My lawyer says there's a good chance they'll drop the charges, and if they don't, that we can plead down to a juvenile misdemeanor. Public sentiment, he says, will be on my side. I'll be in the papers again.

LOCAL TEENS DISCOVER, INVESTIGATE MURDER IN WALKER'S CORNER.

LOCAL TEENS' SLEUTHING LEADS TO ARREST IN SO-CALLED "DISCORD" MURDER

LOCAL TEENS STILL FACING CHARGES AFTER SOLVING GRUESOME MURDER

TEEN SLEUTH HAS A PAINFUL PAST; CONNECTION TO "DISCORD" MURDER VICTIM

GOING BACK TO FINDING THE BODY—

I cut Detective Pera off; I'm not trying to be rude but . . . "She has a name," I say.

"The day you found Miss Sutton," Detective Pera corrects smoothly. "I'm still not clear why you didn't call 911. Or Detective Cho's daughter. Or why you didn't tell anyone."

My mother's hands are strong but softer now. "Does it matter why?"

"If we take this case to trial, yeah. It's gonna matter."

I've tried to be precise, my whole life, about what amount of truth I'm telling at any given moment. I've tried to be very explicit with you. But that assumes that I actually know. There are those times when I don't realize I'm lying to *myself.*

So I'm not sure what to tell the detective, but I try. Okay.

Where do I start?

I told you in the beginning that everything that happens next is both because and not because. I'm not a prism. That moment doesn't flow into me, then separate out into a perfect rainbow. I'm a kaleidoscope, and there's more going on than one light or one color. That man happened to me.

But my father also left.

And my mother let me hide.

And I never tried to step outside.

This scar happened to me.

But I only told the story because I had to.

One friend, my Syd, I chose her.

Except I never tried to choose anyone else.

Because choosing someone else

Would mean exposing myself

Again.

And then I did. I let myself be open.

And she was there. And she was glorious.

Hailey is glorious, and I made myself

Vulnerable.

I am a kaleidoscope. Twist me, and a hundred patterns, a hundred shapes, a hundred lights all compete to make up the whole picture, and they're still not whole. They're glimpses. Slices. Excerpts of me, because I am the only thing that is the totality of me. And no one can possibly know everything.

I cover Mom's hand with mine. I hold on, and I know she can't protect me, except sometimes she can. She can't save me, except in the ways that she does. My mother is no more absolute than anything else; she contains multitudes. So do I. So do you. So did Lark.

My chest aches when I draw a deep breath, but I speak anyway. "Because I was afraid. I had a bad experience when I was younger, and I've been afraid of . . . lots of things, ever since. Including the police."

The detective gestures at her face, along the same path my scar takes. She asks, without asking, if this is the bad thing.

This isn't the first time someone has gestured at their face. Drawn a line, as if they could wear my scar—as if speaking with hands is gentler than speaking with words. But this is the first time that I answer and I don't feel the cut all over again. It's the first time that I open the box on purpose.

Unpack it. Deliberately.

And say, "Yes. I was nine. He asked me if I wanted to see something that would make me feel good in the summer."

Detective Pera flinches.

But finally, I do not.

THAT NIGHT, AFTER MY SHOWER, I SETTLE ON MY bed with my mom's laptop. (The cops took mine, even though I told them there was no evidence on it.) I have to install Skype because Mom never uses it. I hope that Syd still has it on her phone.

I haven't heard from her, but to be fair, she could have called, could have texted. My phone could be ringing right now in evidence lockup, and I'd never know about it. So, with a towel wrapped around my head and another wrapped around my body, I lean against my headboard and position the screen so the camera only catches me from the shoulders up.

(I know what webcams can see now.)

After signing in, I scroll the contact list. Double-click on Syd. Type, *You around?*

I close my eyes. Leaning my head back, I let the laptop rest on my thighs. A bleep, a vibration: just come on already. I know she must be out there, somewhere. A chime sounds, and a message appears.

Ava, what the hell, are you okay?!

My hands hover over the keyboard. The answer is no or maybe even, *No, but possibly I'm going to be*, but I know that's not what she wants to hear. Instead, I tell her, *I'm okay. At home on Mom's laptop.*

The screen shifts; the video stays dark but Syd's trying to make a voice connection. I accept, and turn off my camera, too. I don't need to stare at myself, and she doesn't want to see me. Fair enough. Last time we talked, we screamed. It was ugly. I was ugly.

Even though the camera's off, I see Syd clearly in my mind. She's wearing sleep shorts and her Rikers Island Swim Team T-shirt (an item that made her mother laugh *and* forbid her to wear it outside the house).

Her fingers are splayed out, and she's trying to type without screwing up the last coat of her fingernail polish. (She'll fail. She always does. Syd doesn't have accent fingers. She has do-overs.)

Her room is cool—as in cold: she always has the window open a little—and chaotic. All of Syd's phases remain, so there are tiny blown-glass horses on her dresser from third grade and old posters of Niall Horan from eighth on the walls.

The incense burner appeared when we were thirteen. In Bollywood shades of teal and sea and sunshine, an Insta-ready canopy hangs above her bed—circa last summer, when I was at my dad's and Syd's stepdad started buying her affections.

I could find my way through her house in the dark. She's just as at home in mine. But something has changed, and we're both pretending it hasn't. Our shallow conversation keeps us from drowning in the deeper one we both know is coming.

Because today is about reckoning, I go ahead and say, "Sooooo . . ."

The dark screen flickers, and then there she is. Not as I imagined.

She's got her hair-dying turban on, and out of reflex, I start to ask her what color this time. But that's just not the conversation we're supposed to have right now.

"Yeah, so," she says. "I guess this means you're not in jail. Which is good. I would have had to break you out, and then we'd have to go on the run or whatever. Dude, I don't even know where to start. Um."

Her eyes flick away. It's like she's trying to find the right words. Like they're there, behind her gaze but out of order. Or rude. Or just not exactly right. The video cuts abruptly. She's giving herself a chance to think.

Careful, I keep the camera angled up. It's a nice up-the-nose shot, but one that doesn't make it look like I'm nakedly video chatting my bff. I say, "Yeah, no, I'm not in jail, but I'm still sort of under arrest? I have a court date, anyway."

"For what, exactly?" she asks. "Everybody's talking; nobody knows anything. I even spoke to Hailey."

Her name is an arrow in my flesh. I can absolutely believe that Syd would seek her out, but I know she hated doing it. A vague weight of guilt settles on me, but I can't do anything about that.

For the third time, for the fourth time—I'm not even sure anymore—I start at the beginning and just tell the story. I talk right up till this moment, and then I take a deep breath to exhale.

"And, lucky me, I'm definitely going to a shrink. Mom's making an appointment."

"I can't believe you didn't tell me any of this."

Shaking my head, I say, "I didn't tell anybody. I couldn't. And you've been so mad at me. . . ."

There's a pause. Then Syd looks into the camera—into me. She's serious and earnest, two things she avoids as much as possible. "I love you."

"I know," I say. "I love you, too."

Another long pause, and then she goes on. "No, I mean I love you. I'm *in love* with you. So, um, I'm glad you're okay, and I'm like . . . I can't even believe all this. And I don't want to make things worse, but I think we have to friend break up for a while so I can get my head together."

I slide off the bed, cradling the laptop as I go. I wait for the "Gotcha," the "Prank, biotch!" And they never come. The towel around my hair slips off. I look like a damp madwoman in my little thumbnail at the top of the screen. "Whoa, whoa, whoa, wait, though. What? You can't just say that, and then say that, and . . . what?!"

"It's been a really long time," Syd says. She looks small and soft, as if she peeled out of her shell armor. She is exposed, and this almost never happens. "It was a crush, and I thought it was going to go away, and it didn't. And it was fine. Mostly because I thought you were ace. Like, panromantic, obviously, but also kind of not in play. You were never into anybody, and I was like, 'Okay, I can just love her like this, and it's fine.' It just got harder, and I felt better when you were gone this summer. And then Hailey happened, and you were all about her, and I . . ."

Syd puts her phone down for a second. All I see is her textured ceiling and the whirl of fan blades. When she raises the camera again, she says, "I always thought if you ever were going to fall for somebody, it would be me. And it wasn't."

The video cuts off again, and I feel a bright, fresh pain in my chest. This is the secret she's been keeping from me. From this springs unspoken breakups and unshared tattoos. This is where a silent summer was born; it's what makes Syd bitter and jealous and hard to read. Shame on me; I should have realized it.

This is exactly the way she was the last time her heart broke. I stroked her hair and scooped her ice cream and did all the things a best friend is supposed to do to make it all better. And this time, I can't make it better. I'm the thing making her worse.

Leaning closer to the screen, I say, "Syd. Oh my god. I don't know what to say. I'm so, so sorry. I never meant to hurt you."

"You didn't," she says as she pops back into view. "I did. You were oblivious. Which sucked, by the way. And I suck for saying it sucked. Jeezus, it's just stupid. It's all stupid, Ava. I don't know why everything has to be so hard. I swear, I'm not telling you this to make you feel bad. I just . . . it's . . . *I* feel bad, and I have to change something. All I can really change is me."

Syd's anguish and resolve unfold. There's no hesitation. Something inside me breaks again. It wells over, spilling out pain because she's *practiced* saying this, and I want to ask her how long. How long has she felt like this?

But that doesn't belong to me. It shouldn't. And I can't ask her to give me a chance, because I don't feel that way about her.

Rasping nails and grasping fingers dig down inside, turning over all my emotions, and it's just not there, I love Syd, but I'm not *in love* with her. I'm not attracted. If I could make it happen, I would. I really would.

Those things, I don't say, either. My tears, I swipe away before I respond. For a brief moment, I hate the vanity of this app. That I see my own face imposed next to hers, that I'm not sitting across from Syd and holding her hands and trying to make this better.

Instead, I'm trying to hide my blotchy skin and my red nose by shifting into shadow. I'm crafting my response so it sounds smarter than I am, braver than I am. More generous, more everything. Just better—better than I am, than I really am, because right now, I just hurt, and I know it's not about me, but it feels like it's about me.

"Is there anything I can do? Besides leave you alone, I mean. Because I'll do that. For as long as you want me to or need me to. God, I don't know how to not be your friend, Syd."

"We're still friends," Syd answers immediately. She's shifted into shadow, too. She's still beautiful in silhouette, still bright like the moon, still shooting stars and distant lightning. Her voice is thicker; she's stuffy. "We just have to be friends who don't talk to each other for a while. I'm not giving you up. It's just a break."

Junior year has barely started, so that gives me hope. It's not like we're flowing into college this spring, currents drifting in two different directions.

There's still time. Time for Syd to heal, and time for us to go ranging again. Time to make more memories to go with the *decade* (plus!) that we already have. I'm going to believe in time, because I already miss her.

"I can do a break." Not that it's up to me. I have to; to keep my best friend, I have to give her up for a while. I force a smile because I do want her to feel better. I just wish leaving wasn't the cure. "But if you need me . . . you know where to find me."

"Jail, right?" she asks, and her joke is choked with tears.

My reply is, too. "Yep. The last cell on the block, that's me."

Syd turns off the camera again. She hates it when people see her cry, even me. I guess now especially me. I hear her breathing, but she says nothing. My heart squeezes tighter and tighter, in hard, ugly anticipation of a goodbye. Fear that that *was* our goodbye.

The chat window pops up again. She types, X*OXO*, then signs off. That's our break. That's how we say goodbye.

For now.

It's not so much that they bury her twice, but this is her second grave. The stone is grey, which, good. She was afraid they'd go with pink granite and carven hearts and one of those stupid picture inserts that turn green and strange. It's simple and it's right, and it says:

LARK LORRAINE SUTTON
JANUARY 15, 2002 - OCTOBER 15, 2019
TAKEN TOO SOON

Her father chose the sentiment; her mother chose the clothes she wore in the closed casket. That's silver aluminum, by the way. When the funeral director showed her parents the wood-grained ones, her mother cried and her father stood there awkwardly, next to a woman he divorced years ago.

The weather cooperates with the funeral. There's no light in the sky and no golden beams to contradict the occasion. The little garden cemetery is close to the city but pastoral. Trees, ordinarily tended, stretch out leafless limbs and shade nothing.

To her surprise, a lot of people come. A bunch of people from the school she dropped out of, including two teachers. English and algebra. She doesn't even remember liking their classes that much. But they're there, with black umbrellas that they share with their students.

Her internet peeps are here. Some she already met, and some who would have been next on her list. They stand out because most of them wear jeans and T-shirts, shirts with game logos on them. Rust is there, and so is Minecraft. Overwatch is represented, and Fortnite, too.

The girl who found her isn't there. That stranger who kept her and helped Nick, and made sure Zach Pelletier (so hard to think of him that way; he's still OhWeeOh to her, will be for eternity) got what was coming to him. Her presence would be strange, so not missed.

Nick is missed.

She has so many regrets, and one of them is Nick, wearing an ankle monitor. Nick, who can't leave the state to see her buried properly, who would have given her a place to stay forever. Who knew forever might never come.

It's not right. It's not fair. Life isn't fair. It begins unexpectedly, and the end is either eons away or two seconds after the first breath. Life is chaos, and living is making a path through it. Making a better path, hopefully. Leaving signposts for the people who follow.

The preacher droned on. And where did they find a preacher? she wondered. They never went to church. But there was this small bald Black man, reading from the Bible over her second grave.

The words were fluid and beautiful, written in a language that was meant to be plain and clear. But history is written by the present, and Shakespeare isn't bawdy anymore. King James' plain-word translation is now traditional and melodic and foreign.

But the preacher spoke the truth, and that was comforting.

"Whereas ye know not what shall be on the morrow. For what is your life? It is even a vapour, that appeareth for a little time, and then vanisheth away."

For a few days, she was a vapor, the rattle in the night, the face in the mirror. She was the shape in the shadows, and the girl in the woods. She was Jane Doe—no one and everyone. She watched Ava Parkhurst and loved her a little and led her to grace.

So all that is left is to vanish away. To be no thing on the earth and ash deep inside it. It's a last lingering thought that it might have been better if someone had put her ashes in a rocket and shot it toward the moon. Or spilled her out on the ocean to become part of the sea.

But what is best is that it's done. She is done, and she is light, and nothing hurts. It matters less, matters most.

All is quiet.

All is good.

WINTER WENT AWAY AFTER THEY TOOK LARK HOME.

It got so warm that the trees stopped changing colors. The newspaper was full of people complaining about the Fall Color Festival being a Fall Brown Festival. They just replaced the complaints that the early winter had ruined things first.

Personally, I think that means there was never supposed to be a festival this year. But I'm not the one selling driftwood signs and autumn wreaths to tourists, either.

It's almost too warm for the coffee I bought at Wescott's. Curling the cup against my chest, I walk with my shoulders straight and my head down. I am, after all, "Teen sleuth with a painful past; connection to 'Discord' Murder Victim." They didn't run my school picture with that article, but they ran it with all the others.

And Walker's Corner is a small town. Not crazy small, but people talk. People who already knew me know me all over again. I'm still *the girl with the scar*, but mostly, *I'm the girl who found the body*. This time, people don't avoid me. They don't whisper about me. They walk right up and ask.

What was it like?

What did you do?

Were you scared?

So again, I tell the story because I feel like I have to. But this time, I also want to. I want people to know that Lark Sutton was here. That she's not *the body, the dead girl, the murder victim.*

She's a girl who loved video games and hated her house and went on a grand adventure. She was brave and foolish, and out of all the people she met, only one had a dark heart.

The statistics are in the favor of goodness. If there was a .25 percent chance of rain, you'd leave the house without an umbrella. And if it rained anyway, it's not like you made it happen.

It's not Lark's fault that Zach Pelletier murdered her. It's not my fault that the Summer Man lured me away with lies. It's not your fault, that terrible thing that happened to *you*—it's *not* your fault.

I believe that more completely, more fully, than I ever did before. I believe it now into my soul and my bones.

And I believe what my new therapist tells me. That people are more than the things they do in the dark. That they do in shame. That they hide from and hide inside.

I can't say I enjoy therapy, because I don't. Honestly, I hate that Dr. Hernandez makes me do affirmations

(I am not broken, I am healing.

I am not bad, I am complicated.

I am not a basket case, I have PTSD.

There is nothing wrong with me, and a lot right with me.

I am more than my trauma.)

and checks to make sure I'm keeping my journal and wants me to talk to myself more than I already do. I'm supposed to reassure myself when I'm upset, and congratulate myself when I do well, and, of course, talk down those unwanted thoughts that come unexpectedly. I hate all of it, but I do it.

And when I do it, I feel stupid, but when I feel better . . . well, I keep going. I can open my boxes and sort through them like cataloging terrible souvenirs from nightmare vacations. But then I can close those boxes again, gently. I can settle them so they don't rattle and explode so much.

I still don't like trees close to buildings or holding hands with my pinkies trapped inside. But the nice thing is Dr. Hernandez says I don't have to. I don't have to like tapioca pudding, and I don't have to like things that make me uncomfortable. I have permission to be what history made me.

But I have permission to interpret history as a victor. I survived. I get to decide what it means.

And sometimes, it's terrible. Walking through school and seeing Syd with a new SO, and I don't get to ask about them: terrible. Knowing she's on the same lunch block and sitting tables away from me: terrible.

All the quiet that is left in her wake, it's terrible. But it's better for her, and I tell myself (affirmation!) that loving somebody is doing what's best for *them*, not you.

And I love her. And I want her to be happy. So I keep my distance.

I keep my distance from Nick, too. I'm not supposed to talk to him—we're both witnesses, but we're also co-criminals.

My lawyer and his lawyer want to keep us apart as much as possible, so it doesn't screw up our chances to get charges dropped. He's not my friend, but I do think about him. A lot. We shared something that no one else can ever understand. I hope he's okay.

I walk downtown and don't look in windows. I drink coffee by myself and enjoy the unseasonable weather. It will be seasonable again soon enough. We'll be buried in snow and dark and inside our houses and inside our heads soon enough.

I stop outside Strickland's Gym, and this window, I do look into. There are guys in there, in various stages of lean to buff. I can't hear them, but I can imagine the sweated weight of the air in there and hear their grunts as they press their bodies harder, harder, harder.

My coffee cools, and I drink it anyway. I look at the empty space where I first saw Hailey in beast mode. Those weights rest in their racks, lusciously organized by weight and size. I like the way they all belong. It's beauty in a place we're not supposed to see it.

Probably for too long, I look inside. Those weight lifters probably think I'm creeping. After a bitter swallow of lukewarm coffee, I turn to throw the cup away.

"You ruined it!" Hailey says, her smile like bronze in sunshine. "I was sneaking up on you!"

"Shoulda sneaked faster," I say, and we fall into each other. It's a hug, a kiss, a captured moment of belonging. And when we shift, we're still arm in arm, hip to hip. Her warmth bathes my skin, and her smile lifts my feet from the ground.

"Are we still going?" she asks.

Already, we're walking toward the candle store. We fit together like we were made to, but we also work on it. Her parents don't love me. Big surprise. And she had a moment after she found out what I'd been hiding. Can you blame her? I don't blame her. I didn't say anything about *a body*.

But she's giving me a chance. And I'm being as honest as I can about everything. That meant telling her that I need our hands to fit together another way because of Him. And sometimes, I have to stop, even though she's soft and beautiful and her mouth flows like honey, because I have to get the thoughts out of my head. I am complicated, but she's complicated, too.

Everyone is complicated. We all have our labyrinths and locked doors.

I steal a look at her and tease, "You're not going to narc on me, are you?"

She squinches her face and growls, and it's honestly the cutest thing I've ever seen. Fierce kitten with sweater paws. I look at her and I go dazed and glazed and stupid. I hug her closer and press a kiss behind her ear. We haven't said LOVE yet, but I think we're getting there.

The alley isn't as frightening with Hailey on my arm. And the warehouse is just as fascinating to me with her in it. When I introduce her to Amber, Hailey gushes over her art (on the walls) and her craft (on my skin), and for the first time ever, I see Amber blush.

Hailey sits with me as I settle into the chair. She squeezes my hand and watches Amber build the machine with me. Her eyes go wide when it's time to put needle to skin, and she whispers in my ear, "Does it hurt?"

"Yes," I tell her. "But I can take it."

And with smooth, stark lines, Amber traces a new shape into my flesh, on the inside of my wrist. It's the first tattoo I'll have that other people will be able to see. And this time, I didn't pluck it from celebrity skin.

This tattoo is mine, only mine. I am stronger. I am braver. And this will remind me that I can come back from anything. It will remind me that I'm never alone.

When I look up, I don't see her in the mirror. But I know that she's there.

There, above the faint blue lines that trace my heartbeat, Amber paints three snowflakes, the long reach of a bare branch, and balanced on its tip, a lark.

AUTHOR'S NOTE

This book was incredibly hard to write. Ava's rape is my rape; I've told the story before. The only part fabricated is the scar—my Summer Man only left the invisible kind.

I tell this story because I can, and because it forces people to confront the facts instead of the loopholes. I tell it for my siblings in this terrible trauma who can't. And I used it in this book so I wouldn't be adding one more fictional rape to a world that uses it far too often for entertainment.

My heart breaks for every survivor of sexual abuse and assault, and there are far too many of us. Thirty-five percent of heterosexual women; 44 percent of lesbians, 61 percent of bisexual women. Twenty-nine percent of heterosexual men; 26 percent of gay men, 37 percent of bisexual men. Forty-seven percent of transgender people.

Those of us who can speak up must continue to fight for better laws and better trials for survivors. We must fight to end the backlog of rape kits that have yet to be tested.

We must fight the idea that rape is a moment that ends. That may be true for the predators, but it's not true for survivors. We live with this for the rest of our lives; that moment lives on in our flesh.

We must fight for parity, because rape disproportionately affects the lives of queer people and people of color. We must fight for better rape education, and we must be clear when we discuss consent.

We must love, and support, and uplift each other. We are members of a monstrous association, but we can use that connection for good.

Most important, remember that you must take care of yourself and your mental health first. You don't have to tell your story; you don't have to call your representatives. With time, you may want to, but you never, ever have to.

Your story belongs to you, and I tell mine so you don't have to.

Yours always,
Saundra

HELPLINES

If you are a sexual-abuse or assault survivor and you need help, please reach out. You do not have to do this alone. You do not have to try to get by. Help is available if you need it.

United States
RAINN
www.rainn.org
24/7 National Sexual Assault Hotline: 800-656-HOPE (4673)

Canada
SACHA
www.sacha.ca
24/7 Sexual Assault Helpline: 905-525-4162

England and Wales
Rape Crisis England & Wales
www.rapecrisis.org.uk
Support Line, Open Daily: 0808-802-9999

Scotland
Rape Crisis Scotland
www.rapecrisisscotland.org.uk
Support Line, Open Daily: 0808 801 0302

Ireland
RCC The Dublin Rape Crisis Centre
www.drcc.ie
24/7 Helpline: 1800-77-8888

Australia
1800RESPECT: National Sexual Assault, Domestic Family Violence Counselling Service
www.1800respect.org.au
24/7 Support Line: 1800-737-732

New Zealand
Safe to Talk/He pai ki te kōtero
www.safetotalk.nz
24/7 Helpline: 0800-044-334